The
Growing
Season

By Kip Parker

Prologue

The first time I saw the old woman, she was sitting on a stump in front of her cottage, feeding sticks into a roaring fire. I was puzzled that she knew my name. I thought it the trick of an old huckster. Her plain black dress and colorful shawl reminded me of the picture of Hecate on one of the cards in my tarot deck. And of every so-called gypsy tarot reader I had ever seen on any corner in New York.

I had almost decided that the wily old woman had seen a young Americanski coming down the path, and was ready to make a sale. The beady eyes glinted up at me, as she looked me over. I was waiting for her to tell me that she could teach me all the mysteries, and then name her price. She never did.

I had been tramping around Europe on a wild chase to find my spiritual beliefs. In the anonymous program I had joined, they kept telling me that I had to find a "higher power". But I could not (and still do not) accept their version of a bearded old white man as creator and judge. So I took off in search of something more: something bigger, something older...something that looked more like me. I do not know which I had less of: money or sense. It was a close call. But there I was, somewhere in the dark woods of Europe.

She said to me "Things have not always been as they are now. Nothing is, as it seems. The world is much older than most people think. And The Mother has been with us always. But to see her, you must have the eyes."

I ended up staying there for several seasons, and listening to the many stories she had saved up. She said she was The Rememberer, the last of her tribe. She said she was one of the "Hesh-taz". I asked whether she meant she was a follower of Hestia. She laughed, saying that on the contrary, Hestia was a descendant, named for the group, which was apparently several thousand years older.

Over the course of the next several seasons, and in subsequent years of research, I learned that the Heschtas were actually members of a group of advisors and protectors of the Tribe's leaders (then called Hearth and Hunt Queens), similar to those to whom we refer today as Guardians.

I look back with great fondness on the years I spent with the old one, sitting around her fire and learning how she and her ancestors lived.

In these books I relate some of the tales she told me around that fire. I cannot tell them all. I made a vow. But I do remember. It has been many years since I last saw her. I suppose she has passed over by now. I guess that makes me The Rememberer.

But these books are not intended to be the story of a writer. They are the story of a culture. My culture. Maybe yours, too. Only fragments of pottery and little fat female statues remain for our scholars, like Gimbutas and Monaghan, Reger and Gage to try and piece together.

But aside from the archaeological fragments, there are also fragments of memory. Memories that flirt with us in the dark at the Michigan night stage. Memory that makes us all want to stand together and howl when the moon is round on rocky hills in Ireland or Germany. Memory that inspires us to create theories about who and what we are channeling. Racial memory perhaps? Maybe. Maybe one day, with a few helpful hints, we will all remember. May the Great Bear Mother grant it.

Spring 3778, B.C.E.

"Jori! Do not go there!" Garnet called as she approached the riverbank. "You know you aren't supposed to get your shoulder wet for several days, remember?"

"Don't worry so, mother." Jori squinted up at her, grinning. The insistent cold of the water seeped into the skin of her legs as she stood, slightly bent, ready to scoop out the next hapless fish that swam past. Her feet, however, were warm because they were ankle deep in the soft mud of the river's bottom. "I have not forgotten. I will not go deep enough to wet it. And the pad Anna put on it is still there. I just want to catch some fish for dinner."

She spared a moment, glancing under the bandage at the mossy padding that Anna had used to cover the salve on the new tattoo. She was keeping it clean, as instructed. The salve was thick and smelled like the riverbank, and the wound still itched. Anna had said it was healing well, and would look fine.

The three interwoven crescent moons were the symbol of the Heschtas, the Guardians of the Hearth Queen. Jori could still hear the echoes of the drums that played on her night of initiation, when she had been required to recite the code of the Heschtas, the names of the relics, their uses and their makers, as well as the duties of a Heschta. She shook her head to clear it.

Garnet eased herself down onto the grassy

bank, watching. Jori tossed the first wriggling fish to the shore. "So, how are you doing? I have not seen very much of you lately." There was another splash and another thud.

"They do keep me busy!" Jori laughed, not taking her eyes from the surface of the water. "Tonight I am helping cook. And as much as I love the smoked fish that Wren makes, I was hungry for some fresh." Splash. Thud.

The day was clear and warm. The sun felt good on Garnet's face. She was glad that this winter was finally over: it had been a long and sad one for the tribe.

"That does sound good." Garnet admitted.

The ripple of muscle across Jori's shoulder blades mimicked the ripple in the water as she snatched the unwary fish from their homes to send them sailing through the air. Jori had always been a strong girl, but over the past winter her body had shed the roundness of childhood in favor of the long sleek muscle and curve of womanhood. She would never be as tall as Devin, but she would be just as muscular.

"Shall I get you some, too? Jori asked, snatching another fish from its home.

"Not today, dear." Garnet knew what Wren had planned for the meal this day. "But thank you."

Jori trudged out of the river and climbed the bank to sprawl next to her mother, rubbing circulation back into her legs. They sat in companionable silence for a while, enjoying the sun and the company.

"Are you still worried that I took the oath too soon?" Jori turned, looking directly into her mother's eyes.

Garnet shook her head, and smiled. "No, darling. I am sorry if I said anything that hurt you. I am feeling like the world slips from my grasp lately."

"How so?"

"I went for a long walk yesterday, and realized that I had simply been missing the days when you were little and would hide under my skirts. You can attribute it to the moods of a mother whose children outgrow her."

Jori pulled her mother into a comforting hug. "I will not leave you," she reassured her softly. "But my duty calls me now, and I must strive to be ready."

Garnet rested her head on the big shoulder for a moment longer. When had this young scamp become wise, she wondered? "I am proud of you, Jori," she said aloud. "Even when I do not act like I am."

"I know, momma. There is much sadness still in the tribe. To lose two in one winter is hard, and one of them so young. And it fell upon you to comfort and console everyone. That is a heavy burden, even for you."

Garnet wiped the wetness from her eyes. "Kelan has been a great help to me."

"Would you like to come and stay with me in the Heschtas' hut for a time? Maybe that would comfort you." Jori offered. "I know that no one would mind. They enjoy your company as much as I do."

"I would love to spend some time with you, Jori, but I cannot. The entire tribe feels the weight of sadness. Devin and I must decide how to help us all recover."

"But how can you carry everyone until you have healed yourselves?" Jori's tone became persuasive. "You cannot share water when the cup is dry, mother. Perhaps you and Devin should go off together for a few days; just the two of you."

"I will think on it, dear. And I will talk it over with Devin." Garnet looked out over the water. "Do not worry about us. You have your studies. Concentrate on those." she patted Jori's leg comfortingly as she started to rise.

Jori stood, too, and impeded her mother's escape, enveloping her again for a moment in a soft embrace. "I will not worry if you promise to send for me if you need me." She hooked one finger under Garnet's chin and looked into her eyes. "Will you?"

Garnet smirked. This one was so much like Devin that she could almost mix up their names. "All right. I will send for you if I need you. And thank you, Jori. You are a comfort to an old soul." She planted a soft kiss on the tanned cheek and strolled toward the village.

Jori watched Garnet's stately stride recede. She knew that her mother would not speak of her own feelings to many people. It was part of being a leader, she had taught the girls, to show a calm and positive demeanor even when she felt turmoil. She only revealed her fatigue and sadness to Jori in private. Jori smiled, feeling protective and proud. Garnet liked to lead gently and by example. And it had worked with Jori. Often, when she found herself in a new or difficult situation, she knew how to behave by imagining what her mother would do.

After cleaning the fish, Jori gathered them up and put them into the bag she had brought. She slung the pack over her shoulder, smirking at her own folly. That bag had taken her two whole days to weave from dried grasses! By the time it was done, she had been so frustrated she could barely speak. Usually, she was agile and nimble. But for some reason, her fingers just would not make the right motions to make a tight weave. When Marjika had at last approved the final product, Jori had thrown it down and gone out for a long run beside the river. She could not stand the sight of it any longer. It was Astaga who had insisted that she bring the bag today. And now that it was being useful and convenient, Jori felt more kindly disposed toward it. Yes, she thought, it may have been worth the effort after all.

As she approached the Heschtas' fire, Daña's little daughter ran toward her, black hair flying. Jori scooped the child up and swung her in an arc, restoring her to her feet with a thud only after receiving a smile and a kiss. The child, laughing giddily, ran away. Jori dropped the bag and sat down near the fire.

"So? What did your mother have to say?" Nita had approached in total silence. Jori admired her stealth.

"Oh, she just wanted to see me, I think. Her duties are heavy upon her just now." Jori poked at the fire with a long stick. "Not that she likes to admit it."

Even though the conversation had been a private affair, Jori knew that she could speak of her mother's fatigue with the Heschtas. It was their duty to see to the health and wellbeing of the Queens.

"Indeed." Nita knew Garnet well. "She has spent the entire winter comforting people."

"I suggested that she and Devin go on a walk for a few days. But she said that they could not." Jori used the long blackened pole to move a burning log to the center of the fire, and then added another.

"That is not a bad idea." Nita said slowly, rubbing her chin, "They could use some time alone. I will speak to the others over our meal." Nita looked at the bag Jori had thrown near the fire. "You brought fresh fish?"

"Yes. I like smoked fish well enough. At least I did last fall." Nita smirked wryly at the comment. The tribe had existed on smoked meats and fish for the entire winter. "I was hungry for some fresh today. And you did give me the morning to do as I would."

"That I did. And you chose to use your free time to feed us all." Nita shook her shaggy gray mane. The girl was a natural leader. She thought of others constantly.

Jori snorted sardonically. "I used it to feed fresh fish to myself. But if I bring food, I must bring enough to feed all who will eat at the fire. I am just lucky that I eat here with you and not at the main fire. Even I could not catch enough fish in a morning to feed everyone there! "

"I will go and get the greens we picked yesterday. Will you put the fish on the fire?"

Jori nodded and began to push the fish onto the roasting sticks.

~~~~

Garnet, walking toward the center of the village, marveled at the growth of both her girls. They were both becoming kind and thoughtful adults. Kelan's training was coming along nicely. She was currently staying with the healer for a time, learning more about that aspect of the tribe's life. And Jori's time with the Heschtas would last only one more turn of the seasons before she spent her season with the tribe's scout. They would make excellent leaders when the time came. Of course, Garnet was in no hurry for that time to arrive. Even during the most difficult seasons, as this past winter had been, she loved her place among the people.

Still, she thought, Jori's idea may have merit.

Garnet admitted, even if only to herself, that she was feeling worn. The deaths this winter had been particularly sad for the tribe. She ruefully remembered the endless hours spent listening to women who needed to speak of their feelings. She felt her throat tighten at the thought and pushed it resolutely away. Not yet, she told herself. Today is not the day to deal with these feelings. She turned her mind toward Marjika's new baby, and the naming she must do today.

As she passed the main fires, she caught the faint sound of footfalls behind her. The sound was muted, as though the person sought to be quiet. But Garnet's keen senses told her who was there. Without turning around, she spoke softly. "I thought you were supervising Falcone's workers this morning."

Devin stopped short, exasperated, and stared at her lover. No matter how quietly she walked, Garnet always knew she approached. Of course, she would never allow her frustration to show up in her tone. "I am. They are resting now." She said casually, "They have just hauled several drags of large stones to the site. I just thought I'd use the time well."

Garnet chuckled as Devin's strong arms hugged her from behind. Devin kissed her neck and whispered, "Do you have a few minutes? We could go to your house."

Garnet shrugged out of the grasp, her neck tingling, "I must admit that there have been a few advantages to having the girls sleeping elsewhere. But I have work to do just now. You will just have to wait until later."

"And what are you up to this morning?" Devin draped a companionable arm around her shoulder and fell into step. She was unfazed by the refusal, being used to Garnet's ways. Devin knew well that patience now would be richly rewarded later.

"I am going to speak to Marjika and visit her daughter. It is time for the child to receive a name. I need to spend time with them so I can get an impression."

Following custom, the Hearth Queen would wait until the new child had survived its first winter before choosing a name and formally accepting the child into the tribe. Some children did not live long, succumbing to disease, or simply choosing not to stay on this plane. The death of anyone was an emotional injury to the Hearth Queen. Images of the two who had passed on this winter flashed before Garnet and her demeanor darkened again. She abruptly stopped walking and laid her head on Devin's shoulder.

"I know, love" Devin said softly.

"I never got to speak the name out loud," she moaned. "Kelan and I both heard it the moment she was born."

Devin stood silent for a moment, allowing her lover to experience the pain and the support of being held.

"Kelan too?" Devin steered the conversation

back to the living. "I did not know she had that kind of gift."

"I have been aware of it for several winters. She heard Micah's name when he was born, too. And remember when she went on her first hunt and fainted when Jori killed the animal?"

"Yes, I remember that. It was the summer before I broke my leg."

"I thought at the time that she may have felt the animal's spirit cry out. She may have been overwhelmed by the contact as it was passing over." Garnet explained.

"I hadn't thought of it like that. I just thought she was afraid of the blood…"

"Yes. We all did, darling. Perhaps that is why she cannot hunt."

"Perhaps so." Devin took her hand and smiled cheerfully. "Now come. You must consider a name for that baby before she begins to talk and names herself."

They walked on at a leisurely pace, heads bent together. They presented such a familiar and happy sight that many smiled as they passed. Garnet let out a burst of laughter as they turned toward the house of Marjika. She gave Devin's hand a warm squeeze. She was grateful for the comfort and support of Devin's love. When they reached the children's house, Garnet kissed her lightly and went inside.

Devin continued toward the storage buildings

where the men sat on the ground, resting from their exertions. The men from the allied Tribe were currently staying at their regular summer camp site, not far from the village. The men's typical travel cycle varied, depending upon the weather and other circumstance, but they always tried to spend at least part of the warm season near the women's Tribe. They were traditional allies and friends, and many of the men had been born to women of this Tribe.

In the women's tribe, when a child came to a certain age, they were allowed to choose whether they would stay with the women, travel with the men, or do something different. Most boys of the tribe chose to travel with the men, often in the company of their own fathers.

Several seasons ago, the men's leader had made an agreement with the Hunt Queen. The men had agreed to help with the physical labor of moving the large stones for the permanent buildings in the summer in exchange for smoked fish, meats and cheeses to be supplied by the women in the fall.

Devin smiled, greeting various workers and friends as she approached Daña.

"One more trip and we should have enough for this building, I think." Daña said, glancing up from the marks she was making in the dirt.

"I think so too. That will be close to the same amount we used for the other buildings of this size." A clatter of noise attracted her attention. Some of the women from the fires were bringing jugs of juices and bowls of stew. Jori indicated the group with her strong chin. "When the workers have eaten, we can start out again. There is time for one more load today."

This spring they were constructing a traveler's house. Now that traders and other travelers were used to the village being here, more and more people were stopping on their way up or down the river. And while the women loved to feast visitors, they had decided that so many people coming and going all spring and summer long was too much of a distraction for the life of the village. They reasoned that if they built a guest's house closer to the river, that travelers and traders could be accommodated without any intrusion into their daily routine.

The pounding of racing feet approached, and they turned to see Ara running toward them. Daña and Devin looked at one another and grinned companionably. The girl was quickly replacing Jori as their little shadow.

"Escape your lessons already?" Daña asked the breathless girl.

"I was dismissed early," Ara tossed her head smugly. "Because I said I would spend the afternoon helping you."

"Well, go and get some food from the fire, and then be ready for a walk. We will make one more trip today." The girl scampered happily toward the central hearth.

"She misses Jori, you know." Daña told her friend. "They have not had much time to spend together since Jori went to the Heschtas."

"I know. Jori complains of it too. Or so says Astaga."

"Remember when you spent your years there?"

"I remember sneaking out of the tent at night to go and sit by the river with you. And I remember all the plans we made."

"Most of them have come true." Daña reminded her.

"Not the one about the water." Devin said, referring to the water delivery system that she had learned about from her friend Uba-kala.

"No, but we'll figure it out some day." Daña patted her shoulder. "You have the sketches, after all."

"You are right, my friend. We will work it out. But first, we must see to the hauling of the stones."

Across the commons, Ara took a piece of flat bread and scooped up some cheese. She stood and watched a group of women kneading dough as she chewed. Such satisfying and simple work, she thought. To work the dough and place it on the big flat stone and put it into the fire, and to be able to see and touch the results.

That was the reason she wanted to be a builder. She wanted to build things so that she could touch the results of her work. Soon she would finish her training and be assigned as apprentice. She hoped to be apprenticed to Daña. She admired Daña's skill and artistry.

And, it would bring her close to Jori. Ara smiled sweetly, thinking of Jori's face. After all, Daña got to work with Devin almost every day, and once Jori was done with the Heschtas and the scout, she would be apprenticed to Devin. And since Devin and Daña spent large amounts of time working together, so would Ara and Jori. Ara knew that when they were young apprentices, Daña had harbored feelings of a romantic nature for Devin.

But Devin's lover was Garnet, not Daña. Ara wondered if Daña had ever felt the same exciting stirrings for Devin that she felt when Jori was close by. If she had, it had obviously gone away. She unconsciously touched the amulet that Jori had made her as she wished that her feelings would never fade. Hearing Devin's call to work, she trotted back toward the crews.

~~~~

The fire blazed merrily in the little children's house. The big single room was clean and very warm. The builders had found a way to color the interior walls in a rich warm red. And then everyone had come one afternoon and made beautiful drawings around the walls in hues of ochre. The big soft bed and the rocking hammock added to the comfort of the place. Every new child stayed here with her mother for a time. This house was positioned in the center of the village, swaddled by the hearth fires and the other common houses. Devin had situated it conveniently so that everyone could offer help to the new mother and become familiar with the young ones when they were still new.

"Now, let me hold this one for a time." Garnet whispered, taking the child gently into her arms. She was seated near the little hearth. Marjika had made a strong tea and they had chatted until the child had awakened from her nap. The baby seemed restless, squirming. Garnet held the child to her chest, humming softly, and she quieted. Rocking gently, Garnet looked up at Marjika, "So, tell me about this little one. Is she a quiet babe?"

"Usually." Marjika beamed indulgently, "But she is not shy about letting her wishes be known. And already, she tries to get up onto her knees. I think she will walk early."

"She is very beautiful. Her eyes are so blue they look like the evening sky. And if her hair coloring stays as dark as this, she will be a striking woman. Is she very vocal?"

"Not unless she thinks you are not paying attention. She speaks with her eyes and her expressions more often. There is a face that she makes that means she is hungry. If I do not notice, then she begins to make noises."

"Would you allow me to be alone with the child for a time?" Garnet looked up inquiringly.

"Of course, dear!" Marjika reassured her. "I will take a walk to the river and give you some time to get to know her for yourself." Marjika kissed the child lightly and left the house.

Garnet looked down, and was pulled into a direct, blue gaze. The child neither blinked nor cried nor squirmed. Time stood still. Silently, Garnet opened her heart to the child, hoping to get a glimpse into the little one's future and personality. Her vision softened around the edges, and the child's face seemed to age, becoming a strong looking woman holding a bow and smiling. Garnet widened the picture and saw children sitting on the ground, holding their little toy bows and learning their first Hunting songs from the dark haired woman. Garnet could see her clearly now, the clear eyes looking down lovingly at her little students. And her shoulder held the Heschtas' tattoo.

"Hello, Stev." Garnet said softly, "You will be a strong one; A guardian of our people." The child smiled and reached for Garnet, grasping a lock of her hair in her little hand. Garnet raised the child to her face until their foreheads touched. "I accept your wishes, my daughter." The child laughed brightly.

Marjika decided to have a naming procession the following morning at dawn for the child. Before the sun's rising, Garnet, Devin and Barde appeared at Marjika's door. Marjika was already up, wrapping the child in furs against the morning chill. Soon

Petrov arrived with the other Heschtas to assist in the ritual.

"Are you ready, Barde?"

"Just give me a signal when you are ready to begin." Barde gave a little bow, smiling.

Garnet guided a nervous Marjika outside, whispering instructions and reassurance. Devin assisted by lining up the rest of the women. As the sun's edge rose over the hills, Garnet made the signal and they began.

"AWAKE AND WELCOME OUR NEW SISTER" Barde's clear voice rang out. "ARISE AND GREET STEV, CHILD OF OUR TRIBE!"

Petrov tapped out a little dance beat, and several of the others shook rattles or gourds. Matra, Marjika's first daughter, carried a basket of little carved figurines for the children. As the procession wound its way through the village, women and children appeared from their houses and joined in. After they had passed around the main hearth once, Barde changed her tune to a chant and motioned for everyone to sing along.

"Welcome, little sister, Welcome Stev!"

Barde led them around the main hearth two more times. Garnet waited at the entrance to the fire circle until all had assembled. She took the child from Marjika and held her high.

"I, Garnet, as Hearth Queen of this tribe, welcome this child into our circle. As a member of our family, she is entitled to warmth at our fires, food at our tables, and shelter wherever we camp.

When she is ready, we will teach her our ways. Within our circle, she will be honored and loved, and we will require her to do what she can to contribute to our life. May the Mother bless this child and all of her future choices? I name her Stev!"

As one voice, the entire tribe repeated the name "STEV!"

Garnet lowered the child, looking for any sign of fear or discomfort. The girl was laughing merrily. She kissed the child and passed her on to Kelan, who stood nearby. Kelan presented the child to each woman and child of the tribe. They would kiss the child's forehead or hands, and say her name out loud. Sometimes an infant wailed throughout the ritual, but not this child. Stev had smiled and laughed and looked into every pair of eyes that approached her.

Finally, Stev was returned to her mother, and they made their way back to the children's house. Upon entering, Marjika saw the little pile of gifts. As was traditional, women and children had left the gifts near the hearth in the children's house anonymously.

In the tribe's view, it did not matter what individual provided for the child, so long as someone did. Every child was a child of the entire tribe. And no matter what, even if her mother died, every child would have a home and the care that they needed.

Marjika smiled as she looked at them. Even though the gifts were given anonymously, she could tell who had made each one. The little carved mother was surely the work of Nita. The tiny bow and blunt arrows must be the work of old Astaga. But the coloring of the arrows was Jori's. The shiny river stones in the amulet bag had the feel of Garnet. And she recognized Kelan's fine work in the pattern that adorned the sleeping fur. Marjika's heart was full of the love of her tribe sisters. Hearing footsteps approach, she turned to see Anna guiding little Matra, her older daughter, inside.

"Oh, thank you for looking after her." Marjika said.

"I am happy to help. She is a good girl." Anna smiled.

"We go home now?" Matra asked, tugging on her mother's robe.

"Yes, little one. It is time to go home." Marjika laughed. In the tribe's custom once an infant was named, it was time for the mother and child to return to their own home. Hearing more voices outside, she looked out the doorway. Jori and Nita were there, chatting.

She smiled, knowing that their being outside the children's hut at that very moment was no coincidence. When they saw her, Jori said, "Do you wish me to help you carry your things back home, Marjika?"

"Thank you, Jori. I will have things bundled up to carry home soon. Help would be welcome."

Late that afternoon, Garnet walked along the

river. The water moved swiftly this time of year, and in places the tree branches overhung the bank. Garnet always felt calmer and more grounded when she walked between the trees and the water. She was thinking of Lia, wondering if there was anything more that could have been done for the woman, when she almost tripped over Tem. Tem had been sitting on the bank under a great tree, playing with one of the little felines who lived in the village.

"OH!" Garnet gasped, startled. "I did not see you there."

"I would have spoken, but you looked far off in thought. Come and sit for a few moments." She patted the mossy bank next to her.

Garnet stretched out, and looked up at her friend. "I was just…thinking. About Lia." The baby cat climbed happily from one lap to the other, her tiny claws catching on the fabric of their garments.

"Garnet, there was nothing anyone could have done for her."

"Maybe. But there was a time when the Heschtas asked me if they should intervene, and I stopped them. Maybe they could have helped her."

"That was many winters past. You could not have known what would come to pass. And she did choose to spend an entire winter with the Heschtas. Lia was acting strangely all last summer. Barde told me that she saw her walking in the woods behind the big trench, talking to herself."

"Why didn't Barde tell me that?" The tiny feline jumped from Garnet's knee as she sat up suddenly, startled by the revelation.

"She just thought Lia was upset by something." Tem explained, picking up the kitten and petting it soothingly.

The cats were the descendants of a gift the Norahjen had made to the tribe's children some years ago. She had found a litter of babies near the river at the summer gathering one year, and had become enthralled with their antics. One of the women from another tribe had told Norahjen that adult cats were great predators of small mice and rodents. Norahjen decided to take them home to the village so they could guard the grain storage.

"It is possible that there are more women in the tribe who saw something that they thought was unusual, but did nothing at the time. No one person saw enough to be sure anything was really wrong, I think." Tem paused, her blue eyes scanning the river bank. "And you are not responsible for her death." Tem reached out and pulled Garnet to her. Garnet allowed the contact.

"Maybe we should have a village meeting and talk about it. If everyone is feeling like I am, we need to talk it through. I will go to the Heschtas and call a meeting for tonight. We can have a bonfire."

"Yes. I think that is wise. How will you frame the ritual?"

"I will ask Kelan to pass a basket around, and tell the women to put their guilt and their fears into the basket." Tem hid her smile. She had succeeded in turning her friend's mind toward a more productive subject. Garnet was suddenly focused on the planning. "We will throw them into the fire and be rid of them."

"Maybe then we can all go on the spring hunt with joy instead of this sadness that has been hanging over the houses." She squeezed Garnet warmly and bent to pick up the kitten. "I will return this little one to the grain hut. Her mother is probably looking for her."

"I should get back to the village and speak with Herta." Garnet replied, giving the kitten one last stroke. Before turning to go, she touched Tem's shoulder uncertainly. "Tem… I.."

Tem patted her hand and nodded. "I know, Garnet. I know. I love you too."

The Heschtas encouraged the idea of a grieving fire, and Jori was dispatched to go and gather wood for a bonfire. She rounded up her friends and asked for their help. The girls were happy to assist, especially because it meant being absent from their assignments for the afternoon.

Ara and Jori took a drag into the woods to look for dead branches and logs. Jena and Riala followed Kelan to the great trench. They would drag bales of the dried grasses and hay that had served as a wind-breaking wall during the coldest part of the winter.

"But Kelan," Jena was still not convinced that this was wise, "The grass wall provides privacy and stops the wind. What will we do when it is all burned up?"

"Wren said that we would use the bales to burn all summer and that we would gather and bale new for next winter." Riala butted in.

"Because dried grass absorbs wetness, it absorbs smell too. It cannot be used for cooking fires, but is fine for bonfires and signal fires." Kelan continued the explanation with a quelling look at Riala. "If we do not refresh the bales, they will begin to molder and smell. Just like the rushes we use for our beds."

They were able to fit two bales on each drag, and they made three trips. When they arrived at the place where the fire would be, Garnet took charge.

"Oh, good. Girls, I need you to make a pyramid of those bales. Leave a hand's width between them."

"What is a pyramid?" Riala voiced the question.

"It is a shape like a mountain, thick on the bottom and thin on top. Here, let me show you. Place three bales in a row here in the center. Leave a hand's space between them. Good."

The girls lined up the bales. "Why leave so much space?" Kelan was confused. "When we build a cooking fire, we only leave half of that between the logs."

"The flames need room to breathe. And the amount of space you leave between them will control the heat and speed of the fire. "Garnet was impressed. Kelan asked good questions. "A fire is a living thing, Kelan. Now place two bales on top, covering the spaces. Yes. Like that. And then place one on top in the center. That will make a very good fire." She smiled at the other girls. "Now, go and help Jori and Ara get branches."

Watching her friends trot off toward the woods, Kelan asked, "Mother, when will you teach me how to build a ritual fire?"

"Soon, dear. When you are done with the healers. There are many kinds of fire magic that I will teach you."

"Do you consider knowing how to build a fire to be a magical skill?" Kelan sounded perplexed.

"There are facts about building a fire that any good hunter or traveler or cook can teach you, if you are just building a fire for cooking or warmth. But when you are building a fire for a ritual, there are other things to consider, as well."

"Like intention?" Kelan's quick mind grasped the idea.

"Yes, like intent. And there is more. I will teach you all of it, though I daresay that you know much of it already in your deep self. You have many gifts, my daughter. If you learn to use them with sense and tact, you will become a great queen." Garnet hugged her tightly.

They looked up, hearing a ruckus from the direction of the woods. Riala walked out of the trees quickly, with Ara close behind her. Ara was gesturing and talking with urgency, and Riala shook her head.

As they approached, Garnet sensed mischief. "What's this? Where is the wood you were sent for?"

"Jori is bringing the drag." Ara said sullenly, giving Riala an angry glare.

Riala was standing near Kelan, whispering excitedly. "What is going on, you two?" now Garnet was annoyed.

Kelan brushed Riala's hand from her shoulder abruptly. "Nothing, mother." There was a hint of distaste in her voice. "Just idle gossip. I will go and help Jori with the drag." Ara sighed with relief, and followed.

Garnet watched as she marched off toward the woods. She arrived at the edge of the trees just as Jori and Jena pulled the drag into the clearing. She took one side of the drag from Jena, pushing her out of the way. Garnet wondered what on earth she had just missed. As they approached, Jori laughed heartily at something Kelan said.

"Here we are, mother." Jori's voice was cheerful, "branches taller even than Nita, as you requested."

Garnet wisely dropped the subject of the girl's strange behavior. Kelan had apparently settled it.

"What you need to do now, "she told them all, "is to stand the branches up, leaning against the bales, like this. Make sure that the fingers of the branches reach toward the ground." She took a long branch and demonstrated. "Not too close together."

The crew worked until Garnet was satisfied with the configuration. Then Garnet explained the final task. The girls surrounded the fire stack and reached in, pulling tufts of straw loose from the bales and laying them in little piles in the spaces between the bottom layers of bales. These little piles would serve as kindling. Once Garnet was satisfied, the girls were dismissed to go and attend their personal errands. Garnet watched them go still wondering what she had witnessed.

She made her way to the Heschtas' house, where she sought out Herta. She accepted a cup of strong tea and explained what help she needed for the village meeting.

"I need a potion for all to drink that will assist them in expelling their grief. I want them to cry and speak about it at the fires tonight, and then be done with it by the time the sun rises. Can you make something that will assist the majik?"

"I think I can add the appropriate herbs to the wine for the effect that you seek." Herta assured her." We will also add some of the Sinmona root for flavor and serve it warm."

That evening, Kelan stood with her mother outside the Heschtas hut preparing for the ritual. She held a basket that Astaga had woven this very day. It was oblong and had a lid.

"When you approach each woman," Garnet spoke slowly, highlighting the importance of Kelan's task. "You will look into her eyes. Try to send a welcoming, inclusive feeling to her. Open the basket only a little, as though you do not want the contents to escape. Smile as the woman places something into it, and shut the basket quickly. Nod to the woman, telling her silently that she is finished with the things she put in there. And move on to the next." Kelan was nodding.

Herta and Jori were close by. Herta asked. "Do you think she should practice on us?"

"I do understand what mother wants, but perhaps we should all prepare for the ritual by placing our doubts and fears into the basket, so that we enter the ritual with clean hearts." Garnet looked at the young woman with great pride.

"A splendid idea." Herta grinned.

And so Kelan approached each of the ritual participants and accepted their deposits into the basket. Fortunately all of the participants were in or near the Heschtas' circle making preparations, so she did not have to walk far. She then asked everyone to join her as she approached the Hearth Queen.

Devin, Jori and the Heschtas made a circle around Garnet and Kelan until all touched. The feeling of safety and loving support overwhelmed Kelan. This was the first time that the power of the combined Heschtas had cocooned the girl like this. She was in awe.

She looked up into her mother's eyes and found them brimming. Gathering her focus, she smiled warmly and opened the basket cautiously.

Garnet closed her eyes. Her hands came up, palms to the sky, until they were level with the basket. Her focus was palpable. Kelan opened the basket a little wider as Garnet turned her hands over, as if spilling salt into a cooking pot. Kelan gently closed the basket's lid as loving arms surrounded them both.

After a few moments, Garnet spoke, breaking the moment. "Thank you, dear ones. We are ready. Let us go and perform our duty now."

The mood of the women had indeed lightened after the ritual. And the Heschtas, after talking it over, had decided to suggest that Devin and Garnet get away from their duties for a few days.

The next afternoon Herta approached Devin at the site of the new building. She spoke of Garnet's fatigue and of her own. "Take her up to the hills to see Toban getting milk from the sheep." Herta advised.

"Lift that one to the corner, just there!" Devin shouted to the men. She turned to Herta, smiling. "Well, the outer walls will be done with this batch. I suppose I could let Daña finish the roof. Ara and Jori would help her, would they not?"

"Jori has already offered. And you know well that whatever Jori does, Ara wishes to be a part of. They will be mates, you know."

Devin stopped in her tracks, startled. "But are they not too young?"

"No younger than you when you first went

hunting alone with Garnet. Herta stopped the protest with a raised hand and a shake of her bushy gray mane. . "Whatever will be, it will be well."

"Hmm." Devin rubbed her chin thoughtfully.

"So will you speak to Garnet?" Herta persisted.

Before Devin could answer, Swain's whistle reached them, announcing the arrival of Falcone. The men had stopped what they were doing to turn and look. Devin shouted for them to finish what they were doing. She and Herta strode down the riverbank to greet the men's leader.

"Greetings, Falcone!" Devin said to him when he was within hearing. "What brings you here?" She was puzzled. He had not visited the village at all this spring.

"I have come for my tribesmen." Falcone announced loudly. "A herd of reindeer have been spotted by our scout, and we must take the opportunity for our spring hunt."

"Ah." Devin nodded wisely. "Yes. If you have a herd in sight, you must not waste the chance. Will you take refreshment while you await them?"

He was guided to the spot that had been set up for the worker's meals. Devin sent word to the men to attend their leader after they had finished what they were doing. She smiled as she saw that one of Wren's apprentices already approached with a jug and a loaf.

"Did you winter well, my friend?" she asked Falcone politely.

"We did not go hungry," the little man acknowledged sourly. "Your smoked fish and meats last a long time into the cold moons. We made a good trade last season. "

"Good. We are glad that our friends eat well and have health in the cold times." She noticed that Falcone's countenance had suddenly darkened. "And the work your men provide is a great help to me. You know, Falcone, over the winter I learned something about meats that could help you."

"What is that?" his eyes narrowed suspiciously. He was scowling now, so she spoke quickly, trying to lighten his sudden mood change.

"A trader came down the river. The only outsider we saw all winter. He told me that the people who live where there is always snow keep their meats wrapped in skins, directly in the snow. He said that if meat is kept in ice all winter, it will last until spring."

He snorted derisively. "You and your fancy ideas. You may think that you are superior, Devin, because of your ideas and gadgets. But you could not have built half of this place without the strength of Falcone and his warriors! You are only women, after all!" He pounded his fuzzy little chest with his palm for emphasis. She looked at him incredulously as the tirade went on. "You think we would starve in the winter without your ideas? All of your ideas would come to nothing without us. Now we must go and do something worthwhile."

He rose haughtily, saying "My men can finish

this day's work for you, because of our agreement. But do not expect their return tomorrow." And he stormed off down river.

Devin's jaw hung open. She had seen Falcone act angry and stubborn before, but this was just ridiculous. What had made him so angry, she wondered?

"Well, the good news is that now you have the time to take Garnet away for a few days." Herta chuckled.

"But..."Devin sputtered, "What did I say to offend him?"

"Only he knows that." she answered, "His logic leaves something to be desired. Always has. Perhaps the tribe he came from looked at the world in a different way than we do. You know, we did not find him until he had six or seven turns. And even though we raised him as any other child of this tribe, he was with his original tribe long enough to absorb their ways."

"Perhaps..." Devin looked out in the direction Falcone had gone. "I had forgotten he was a foundling. Norahjen found him wandering on her way back from the Gathering one season, did she not?"

"Yes. Norahjen said he was stalking her like she was game. She had to tie him onto a drag to get him to come along. He was dirty and skinny and had infected cuts on his legs. Norahjen thought he had been badly used by his people."

"He was always a little....twitchy. But he has

never acted in a manner before that was disrespectful of us. I wonder what happened over the winter to bring out this mean streak in him." Devin looked thoughtful. "I will ask Toban when I see him."

"Well, he will calm down after the hunt. Do not worry. By the time the sun begins to set, the walls will be done anyway."

By the time the sun was high the following day, arrangements had been made for Devin and Garnet to take a long walk. Daña, Jori and Ara were very happy to take over the construction. Kelan would stand in for Garnet, supervising the gardeners and handling whatever came up. The Heschtas, as always, would keep an eye on them all.

The couple started out after mid-day with two of Devin's dogs trailing happily behind. Garnet had not wanted the dogs to follow. But Devin had reminded her that the dogs' presence would be useful. They would sleep near the fire and warn Devin and Garnet if any large animals came near. During the spring there were many animals that were just out of their winter hibernation. That made them surly and hungry, and therefore more dangerous to humans. Devin had drawn a rough map in the sand to show Jori and Ara where the couple planned to go. "So that you know where to start looking in case we get lost." Devin had said, grinning.

"I do not believe that you have ever been lost!" Ara exclaimed.

Patting her shoulder reassuringly, Devin said, "Thank you for your faith in me, my young friend. But I require any small party that goes out to let someone know the route they have picked. Would it do for me to go out without following my own rule?"

Garnet reveled in the comfortable silence as they walked up the river some time later. Occasionally they would speak, pointing out nearby animals or interesting sights. But they had no need to fill every void with words. It was enough to be alone and together.

Well, she thought, we are almost alone. One of the dogs had dragged a dead fish to Devin for her inspection. Devin ruffled the dog's head and threw the smelly carcass back into the water.

She turned to look at Garnet "would you like to have fish for our fire tonight? I can catch a few fresh ones if you like."

"That would be wonderful. Jori caught some the other day for the Heschtas, and the idea appealed to me."

They lowered their bundles to the grass. Devin took off her boots and leggings and waded into the cold water. Jori had made the boots for her from the hide of a reindeer she had hunted. They were lined with fleece that she had bartered for with Toban. And, she had learned from Astaga how to cure the hide on the bottom so it would be stiff and resist puncture by stick or thorn. Devin prized the boots, and took great care of them. She wore them on every hunt and trip away from the village, except during the hottest part of the summer.

Garnet bent near the water's edge, pulling succulent greens to accompany the fish. She hummed softly to herself, happy in the simple task. She looked up, hearing a splash, in time to see a salmon hit the bank. "A big one!" she shouted, "One more should be enough!"

Before they resumed their walk they cleaned the fish. They rinsed the offal into the stream, offering a meal for other fish in return for the ones they had taken. Garnet wrapped the fish in the leaves she had picked and tucked the little bundle away for their evening meal.

Later as they ate, Devin spoke of Falcone's outburst. His imperious attitude had irritated her, and she failed to understand it.

"Falcone has many good characteristics." Garnet paused, smirking, "But the ability to reason is not chief among them. "

"I admit that individually, the men are mostly larger and stronger than the women. But if we did not have the help of the men, we would simply use a larger number of women and build more slowly. I thought that the trades we had been making these last few years were good for both tribes."

"As they have been. You said that even Falcone admitted that the smoked meats lasted him well into the cold moons." Garnet assured her. "They eat better for having traded with us."

"Maybe that IS it!" Devin was excited by sudden recognition, "He has always been the best provider of food for his people. But since he made the trades with us, they have food that did not come from his effort. Of course it was him who made the trade, and so he did provide the smoked meats."

"I agree that his reasoning is flawed, but that could be what he is feeling." Garnet said thoughtfully. "He fears change of any kind because he does not understand it. And because he is leader, he thinks all should share in his opinion. He is lucky to have old Dain to advise him."

"What is he so afraid of? " Devin was incredulous. "Surely no one challenges his leadership."

"I do not know. I only know that he seems to need to be the center of everyone's attention. He seems to need to be seen as the smartest and the strongest man in the tribe. It is almost as if he were still a little boy, needing to be in the middle of the entire world."

"Well, he is of no consequence here." Devin shrugged. "We need him not."

"That could be the very thing he fears most of all. Now, I have something else to talk about."

"Oh?" Devin noticed the change in her countenance. "You look worried about something. What is it?"

"I do not know whether to worry or not. Remember when the girls helped me to build the bonfire the other afternoon?"

"Certainly."

"Well, Jori and Ara were off in the woods, collecting long branches. I sent Jena and Riala to help them. When they came out of the woods, Riala seemed as though she would burst with something. And Ara looked embarrassed. Riala ran to Kelan and they whispered. Kelan was angry with her, and stormed off to help Jori bring the drag back. She even shoved Jena out of her way so she could walk next to her sister."

"Hmm. That is odd. Did you find out what it was about?"

"I persuaded Jena later that evening to tell me. She said that they had seen Jori kissing Ara in the woods. Apparently, Riala wanted to gossip and tease the girls about it. Kelan stopped that nonsense, thank the Mother."

"Good for Kelan!' Devin smiled. "So what has got you worried?"

"Ara is young for it, is she not?"

"Only two seasons younger than Jori. And they are evenly matched in temperament, I think." Devin patted her lover's leg reassuringly. "It will sort itself out. But they DO give me a good idea." Devin reached for her, grinning.

"Kissing in the woods?" Garnet laughed merrily as Devin began to untie the laces of her clothing. Her breath quickened as the back of Devin's hand brushed her skin. Devin leaned closer, looking into her eyes and reaching underneath the garment.

~~~~

Jori squinted, watching the lithe body of the scout approaching. The sun was high and bright. She raised her hand to shield her eyes. Swain raised her hand to her heart in the greeting of a friend and Jori stood, mirroring the signal.

"Ah, Swain." She embraced the wiry scout. "It is good to see you. Have you run far?"

"Not too far." Swain answered, returning the hug. "I have only been running for part of the morning."

"There is still some rabbit stew in the pot. And the rushes of your sleeping place were changed recently, too. Will you stay for a few days?"

"That depends upon your decision, my friend. I have come to report a very big herd coming up the river." She sat down on a stump next to the one where Jori had been carving arrows.

"Oh? On this side?" Usually, the large herds traveled up river on the other side, following the wide flats.

"Yes. Falcone's men must have scared them away from their normal traces. I saw one of their scouts early today. He said that the men had hunted very well. Falcone and his party still have not returned to their village, though. The scout said they had sent the Reindeer back to the village, and that Falcone had taken the rest of his party to the mountains to hunt a great cat for the furs."

"It is still very cold up that high." Jori remarked. "It could take them several days to get to the cat's territory."

"True. And it takes time to stalk a good hunter like that one." Swain commented.

"Perhaps we should prepare for our spring hunt, too." Jori pondered aloud. "What do you think?"

"I would wait for one more sun before setting out toward the herd." Swain advised. "They still sniff the air frequently. One more sleep and they will have forgotten their losses. They may even cross over the river again. It will be easier to hunt them on the flats than in the woods. But it is up to you, Jori. With Devin away, you must decide."

"I will seek the advice of Astaga as well, but I think you have the right of it. For a big hunt, it is better to have an entire day to prepare, and not just part of one. And perhaps Devin and Garnet will return tomorrow and join us. So eat, friend, and rest. There is time."

Astaga agreed with Swain and Jori, and so the plans began. Barde was notified, and she carried the news around the village. She also asked Daña, Tem, Kelan and Ara to come and eat their evening meal at the Heschtas fire so that plans could be made. Jori helped Nita and Marjika prepare the meal of flat bread, cheese, smoked boar and greens. The Heschtas little fire was crowded, but the mood of the women was happy.

"I agree that we should not wait for Devin and Garnet to return before making plans. If the herd is close by, we should act." Tem chewed as she spoke.

"The Mother brings food to our doorstep. To fail to accept the gift would be unwise. Devin would decide the same, I think." Kelan added.

"But we should wait one day for the herd to settle." Swain cautioned.

"Yes, that is well. If the men have just hunted them, the herd's scouts will be nervous. It will be harder to get close to them." Astaga agreed.

"The herd has scouts?" Ara was amazed.

"Yes, my young friend." Swain smiled at the girl. "Adult females walk along the edges of the herd, sniffing the wind for predators. It is the reindeer who taught our own scouts many lessons."

"If you come to my fire on the full of the moon, I will tell the tale of Adiage and the Reindeers." Herta promised.

"Now. If the herd does cross back onto the flats," Jori returned to the main subject, "We will have to approach facing the wind. And we will need a few hunters to circle around the herd and use their scent to push the herd toward the main party." she looked to Tem. "Will you take that part for us, Tem? "

"I will, and I will choose three others to help me." Tem was proud of the way the girl was taking charge.

"Good. And will you join the hunt, sister?" she asked Kelan courteously. Though she thought she knew well the answer.

"I will assist Wren in the preparations for your return, and I will organize the care of the children while you are gone." Kelan told the group. "If our mothers return from their little trip in time they will both want to hunt. And someone should stay in the village."

"You are wise." Jori acknowledged her sister's choice.

"I will see to their hunting tools in case they come home in time to join us." Daña volunteered.

"I am sure they will appreciate that." Jori smiled at her.

The next day was busy with preparation. Everywhere Jori walked, there were women sharpening arrows or stringing bows. She spoke with Wren, whose apprentices were preparing travel food for the hunters. She asked Ara to be sure that the party would have enough empty drags to bring back the meat. Swain had gone out again at dawn to watch the herd. She would report back to Jori before the sun rose the next morning.

Approaching the Heschtas' fire, she noticed Norahjen sitting on a log, whittling. The old scout motioned for Jori to sit down.

"I have wanted to speak with you alone, Jori." she began. "I know your studies are going well, and I am proud of your progress. I need to be sure that you understand the gravity of your decisions today."

Jori felt as if she were a small fish being held by huge hands. Inside, she squirmed. Her face showed no trace of her discomfort, however, as Norahjen went on. "The very lives of the tribe rest on your decisions today. Not just whether we will have meat. But if you lead the hunters into a dangerous situation, one or more could be injured, or even killed. The trust placed in you is enormous."

Jori looked at the ground in front of her feet, knowing that what the woman said was true. "How do I know that my decisions are right?"

"You stop and think, you clear your heart of any pride or fear, and you listen to your heart. Once you have a decision, you consult your advisors to make a plan. You must remain open to the voices around you. Know that while you are usually right, sometimes others can see further than you."

"I give you my word. I will always be mindful of the safety of each woman, and the good of the whole." Jori looked directly into the eyes of the old scout.

"I know you will young one. I have faith in you. Know that if ever you are confused or unsure, you can come and speak with me. I love you and I trust you, and I am here to assist." She hugged the girl for a long moment before letting her go.

By late afternoon Jori was tired but all was ready. She sat leaning on the wall of the great hearth, rubbing a fat mixture into the sinew that served as her bowstring when she heard Barde's voice.

"The travelers are returned!" Barde's good news reverberated happily through the village.

Jori's heart sank. She was glad for the return of her parents, but Devin's presence in the party would prevent her from leading the big hunt out tomorrow. She sighed, putting the bow and the pot of fat aside, and walked toward the house of her mother. She steeled herself to hide the disappointment lest her mother think she was not glad to see her.

Several women had gathered to watch the couple stride jauntily into the village. Garnet looked quite happy, Jori decided. Her stride was loose and long, and her arms swung in a wide arc around her as she walked. They were laughing at something.

"Hello, my mothers" she said as soon as they approached. Garnet pulled her into a tight hug. Her smile came easily. She really was glad to see them.

"Hello, my love!" Garnet cried out, "It is good to be home!" She turned and hugged Kelan, too.

Jori turned to Devin, who threw a companionable arm across her shoulder and asked. "So, young leader, what has been happening in my absence?"

"A herd has come near the village." Jori reported. "I have prepared to make the spring hunt when the sun rises."

"Is it a large herd?" Devin stopped walking and looked down at the girl.

"It is the herd that Falcone's men hunted. They came up river on this side, and Swain has been watching them. We held a planning meeting last night, and all is ready."

Devin glanced at Tem, who was in the crowd. Tem smiled, nodding discreetly. Devin relaxed, trusting her friend's message.

"Well then!" Devin grinned at her. "Your mother and I should go to bed early if we are to follow you out at dawn!"

"Follow…. me…?"Jori stammered, looking from one parent to the other. Her heart raced. Could it be true? Devin would let her lead the big hunt after all?

"Of course, girl!" Devin roughly shook her shoulder. "You have made all the plans. This is your hunt. Your mother and I will enjoy following you for a change."

Jori looked back at her mother, who was beaming, too.

"Have you made preparations for-"Garnet began to question the details of the plan, but abruptly stopped the sentence, as she glanced at Astaga, who was shaking her head.

"Oh, never mind, love. I trust that you and Kelan have done well." Astaga nodded, smiling wisely. Garnet kissed Jori's cheek and then Kelan's, and went into her house.

Jori walked back in the direction of the wall as though she were stunned. She was beyond words. A great flaming ball of enthusiasm threatened to burst in her chest. They would let her lead!

She found Ara waiting near her bow. In her elation, she picked the girl right up off the ground, swung her around in a circle and kissed her before putting her back on the ground.

"They will let me lead!" finally finding voice for the joy.

The next morning, the pre-dawn air had a crisp chill. Muffled voices murmured around Jori. It sounded much like a small brook, she thought. She touched her amulet, hoping that her nervousness did not show. It looked as if the entire tribe had come, although she knew that some would stay behind. Wren and several others would be making preparations to receive the meat. The elders that were able would tend the young children. Barde did not care to hunt, so she would not go. She preferred fishing.

Taking a deep breath to hide her nervousness, Jori made the signal to gather the leaders. Tem, Daña, Devin, Ara and Nita approached her.

"Does everyone know what to do?" she made eye contact with each hunter. She noticed that both of her parents stood at the rear of the circle quietly. She was glad to have such strong support.

Most times, there was one plan formulated for a hunt. But since they would not know until

Swain arrived whether the herd would be in woods or flat ground, they had made two plans.

They chatted quietly until Ara pointed into the distance. Jori turned to see Swain running toward her. She held out her water skin for Swain to drink and then asked, "What of the herd, my friend?"

"As we suspected, they returned to the flats when the sun was high yesterday. They still travel up the river, and they are close by."

"Thank you Swain." Good, she thought. We will not have to travel far to find them.

"Truly, the Mother does bring the meat to our door." Ara said happily.

The hunt went very well indeed. They used all the drags that the tribe had brought, some carrying two animals, to bring back all the meat. The sun was setting before they could see the village.

As they crossed the river Kelan approached the group. One look at her face alarmed Garnet. She signaled to Devin and Jori, and they went to her.

"What is it, Kelan?" Garnet was concerned.

"Oh, mama! A boy from the men's village came as a messenger." She began.

"A boy?" now Devin was alarmed too. The men would never send a boy out with a message unless there was no grown man to send.

"Yes. He said that Falcone and the hunters

had not returned yet from the mountains. The elders ask us to send searchers. They think the men were all lost in the snow." She began to cry. Garnet gently held the young woman.

Devin, suddenly all business, turned to Jori. "You take the meat and lead the hunters back home. Stay in charge and take care of your mother and sister."

Jori nodded. Devin turned to the body of hunters who were waiting patiently near the river's edge.

"Falcone and his men are long overdue from a trip to the mountains. Their elders think a big snow must have surprised the party. I will go and look for them. Will anyone come along?"

Every woman raised her hand or said she would join the search. Devin smiled proudly. She picked out Tem, Herta, Swain and three more. "We will gather what we need and meet at the visitor's house. Tem, will you ask Wren for travel food for a several days, please? And Jori, will you have some drags brought there as soon as they are empty?" She did not say what use they would put to the drags, but the faces around her reflected the grim knowledge. The drags would be used to bring out the injured. Or the dead.

Kelan stepped to Devin's side. "I must go with you," she said quietly.

Devin looked at the girl, surprised. "Kelan, the mountains are too dangerous."

"You will need someone who knows the

healer's ways. And when we get closer, I will be able to find them."

"Find them?" Devin was confused.

Kelan looked to Garnet for permission, and receiving it, went on. "I can feel Toban's presence, even from a distance. When we get up the mountain, I will be able to guide you to him."

Devin looked at her mate. Garnet nodded. "Kelan has many gifts. She is correct. She should go with you, dear."

The women scattered, going to help with the preparations. Devin gathered those who would go with her.

"Go to the hearth fire and eat some food. Then go to your homes and rest for a short time. This will be a much longer walk than the one we just took." she instructed them.

Taking her own advice, she picked up some cheese and bread. She sat on the ground with her back to the wall. She would have liked to go to her own house for a little while, but she felt that she should be accessible in case anyone needed her. Tem approached and sat next to her, munching contentedly on a hunk of the smoked cheese.

"So, the arrogant one is lost in the snow. And we must go and pull him out. This will not sit well with him."

Devin nodded. "It will sit better with him than dying, though. And if it was us out there, Falcone would come."

Tem snorted her skepticism. "You would

never endanger the women by taking them to the mountains before the thaw is over. You would never let wounded pride make decisions for us. I do not know why he was so angry with you when he was here, but it obviously affected his judgment. He is not the great leader he thinks he is. He thought only of his pride, not his people. He has changed as he has grown older. He begins to remind me of Shayana. Perhaps it is time for a younger man to take over."

"Maybe that is true. But it is not an idea that should be repeated to anyone but me. His tribe chooses whom they will follow. And we must go and help them, no matter what our opinion of their leader. Remember this: many of those men were born right here. They are our sons and brothers and friends. "

And so the party went to the mountains. It had taken three sleeps to get to the steeper slopes where they thought the men would be. The higher they climbed, the colder it got until on the third afternoon they were walking in snow. Devin was grateful once again to Jori for her warm hunting boots.

On the fourth day, late into the morning, Kelan asked for a halt. While the party watched from a distance, she held her hands palm to the sky and away from her body. She stood like that for several minutes, eyes shut and swaying softly. The rescuers remained silent, though some fidgeted as the moments passed. Kelan took a large breath and nodded her head definitively. She turned to Devin and said "This way," indicating a direction to her left.

Devin wondered at the girl's close connection to Toban. They had been raised together, it was true, but the young man was not her brother by blood. Devin thought that there must be some other connection between the two young people. She would try to remember to ask Garnet about it. Garnet would know.

The party trudged in the direction Kelan had indicated. When Kelan told them that the men were near, the party made loud noises for a few moments and then stopped to listen. After repeating the exercise several times, they finally heard the men calling out to them.

The entrance to the cave was blocked with snow and big boulders. There was an overhanging ledge of snow just over the entrance. When they tried to start digging, more rocks and ice tumbled down from the cliff. After a short discussion, one of the smaller members of the party climbed up and used the long carry poles from the drags to clear the snow ledge that hung over the entrance. Then they dug out the entrance from the top down until they had an opening large enough to crawl through.

Once a few of them got in, they learned that the party had been trapped when an unexpected snowstorm came up.

Falcone found a cave in which they could wait out the storm, but something triggered an avalanche and the falling snow and rocks covered the entrance to the cave, preventing their escape. The men had been unable to dig themselves out without bringing more snow, rocks and boulders down upon themselves. The big rocks had injured some.

They pulled out the three injured men first, Falcone among them. Devin was grateful that no one had been killed. The men had been very lucky. The thick layer of snow and rock that had walled them in had also insulated the cave against the worst of cold and wind, and so had spared lives. They were hungry and thirsty, and some were injured, but they were all alive.

Toban had tended the injured as best he could during their entrapment. One man had a bad break in his arm, and Toban had realigned the ragged bone and wrapped the arm. Another had a bad cut down the length of his thigh. Both would recover. But Falcone had been hit on the head by a falling boulder, and would not awaken. Toban sought Kelan's council regarding the injury.

She unwrapped the wound and looked closely at it, then opened Falcone's eyes and looked at their color. She checked his breathing and listened to the beating of his heart. At last she looked up at Toban. Her eyes told him that this wound was not one either of them could heal. She held one hand out to Toban, and laid the other over Falcone's now closed eyes. Toban laid his free hand over his father's heart. She closed her eyes and swayed slowly, concentrating.

After a time, she opened her eyes again and said, "His spirit is here, but it is deep within him, covered by a mist. Perhaps old Dain will know a way to clear the fog. But I know not."

"I am sure that Dain does know something, or one of the Heschtas. You are not to blame, nor am I. My father insisted that we go to the mountains even though I counseled against it. He is a stubborn man, Kelan. If there is a way to survive this, he will find it."

She smiled up at him, her heart fluttering wildly. "Thank you, Toban. You always know my thoughts."

The party took the injured men back to their home. The women stayed in the men's camp only long enough to sip some hot soup before returning to the village. Dain had echoed Toban's words, telling Devin that Falcone was strong and would eventually awaken.

Devin fervently hoped that Falcone would be well enough to travel by the fall. If he were not, his tribe would have to leave him in the care of the women until they returned in the spring. She did not cherish the thought of an entire winter with Falcone camped in their new visitor's house. He was a good ally at times, but his abrasive and haughty manner were grating. And he would be annoyed to have been saved by Devin and her women.

Since they had settled here, winters for the tribe had become a time of happy storytelling. It had become a cozy time of reconnection for the big family after the bustle of the harvest. Devin did not want that time disrupted by Falcone's presence. She dismissed the thought, trusting the future to the Mother. She sent up a little prayer that Mother look after them all, and then let the subject go.

~~~~

Jori was learning to make wine. This was tedious work involving a long wooden tool with a wide flat end and a deep clay pot. She stood next to the pot, which was so tall it reached Jori's chest and was filled with softened dried plums. Her arms ached from the constant motion. She looked into the big pot's depths. The sticky mess no longer resembled any fruit she had ever seen, but the smell was unmistakable. At intervals Marjika would appear, pouring water or herbs into the pot with the fruit.

Over the winter months Jori had learned how to make big pots like this one, along with other earthenware tools and vessels. And she had studied the intricate design of the artwork with which the vessels were adorned. She loved the idea that a spiral pattern of bowed lines always meant wind, but that if you made the lines in the same symbol wavy, it meant water flow or river. The complexity and consistency of the logic appealed to her ordered mind.

Today, however, her task was much more physical and tedious. The paste she was making had to be a very specific consistency, according to Marjika. This would probably take all day. Jori busied her mind by reciting to herself the travel song that Herta had taught her last summer.

The song was a very old one that mapped out the route that the tribe had walked, season after season, without much change. This song was the tribe's way of remembering the locations of water and food sources, good caves and camping grounds. Each Queen and scout was required to memorize this song as part of her apprentice training.

Old Herta was in charge of remembering all the teaching stories and songs for the entire tribe. It was her job to teach each apprentice of the tribe the songs that related to the skill they had chosen to learn. Then whatever woman was the teacher of the apprentice would spend time showing her how the words of the song applied to her craft.

Jori wondered how Devin would finally show her the places and things in the travel song? Would Jori and Devin actually walk the route for a season, or more? Well, Jori had at least until next spring before that would happen. She pushed the thought away and looked again into the big pot.

The goo that she was pounding on still held a few plum sized lumps. It was getting smoother as time crawled by. She wished time would scamper, instead. She was looking forward to the morning.

For then, she would rise before the dawn and follow Tem down the river to fish.

Swain had alerted the tribe that a party of traders was approaching the village. The traders would arrive in the afternoon, or so Swain had predicted. So Tem had decided to take a party out fishing in the early day to provide a fresh feast for the travelers. Swain had also said that the party was traveling "on the water". Jori wondered what she meant by that.

At any rate, Marjika had said that if the Plums were ready by sunset today, that Jori could go on the fishing trip. The thought made Jori renew her efforts at pounding the mush in the jar.

Jori's excitement awakened her before it was light. She rose and silently left the house, taking care not to make any noise that would awaken the women sleeping there. She quickly washed her face and ran toward the river's edge, where several women already sat talking.

She felt a surge of warmth radiate up from her center as she recognized Ara among them. She stopped walking mid-step. Her palms tingled, and she could not tear her eyes from the sight. Ara was laughing merrily, her eyes dancing and her hair shining softly in the morning light.

A friendly slap on the shoulder jolted her awake.

"Good morning." Devin grinned.

"Uh-good morning." she stammered.

"Pretty, isn't she?" Devin asked, walking past Jori and heading toward the fishing party.

"Huh? Who?" Jori felt disoriented. She shook herself to clear her head, and followed Devin toward the others. Devin said no more, but smiled at her knowingly.

"Ah, here they are." Tem smiled at the pair as they approached the group. "Ara thinks we should go upstream a little. She has seen the bears fishing in an inlet, and thinks there is a spawning ground there for the fish."

"A good observation." Devin said, nodding toward the girl. "Will you show us the spot?"

Ara's observation had turned out to be correct. A short walk upstream had led them to a place where there was a little inlet along the river's shore. In these quiet pools, away from the current of the river, the big fish lay their eggs. By watching the bears, Ara had noticed that the fish seemed not only plentiful in this little pool, but also sluggish. Tem explained that the fish would hover over a spot for long periods while they deposited their eggs. And this hovering meant that they were slower to react and swim away from hungry hunters.

The party spread out along the shore and began to wade into the water slowly. Within moments, the first wet thuds of fish hitting the shore could be heard. The children who had come with the party were kept very busy gathering up the fish and putting them into the baskets they had brought along.

Jori was standing completely still, watching a big fish swim toward her waiting hands. She held her breath as it came close. One more moment, and she would have it. The moment did not come, however. She was startled by a wet slap on the side of her head. She raised her hands defensively, and caught the fish that had been thrown at her. Looking around, she tossed it onto the shore. There were others near her, but all seemed to be concentrating on the water. Ara, however, had a smirk on her face that told the story.

When they had caught enough for several meals, Tem called them to the bank. As she turned to walk toward the shore, Jori saw Ara ahead of her. She lunged forward, tackling the girl in the water.

"There. Now we are even." She turned to trudge toward shore, only to feel Ara jump on her back.

"Your turn!" Ara shouted, pulling her under the cold water.

Jori found her feet again and shook the cold water from her face and ears. She looked to the bank, and saw several women watching.

"Come now, you two." Devin chucked. "Ara, you are the youngest and so must present the gifts to the Mother."

Jori and Ara took several fish and laid them on the grass near where the bears had been fishing. They walked back toward camp slowly, their heads inclined toward one another.

The travelers arrived midmorning. And, as Swain had said, they were traveling "on the water". These traders had come up the river itself. Jori marveled at this new idea. She looked to the middle of the river where the traders stood on a flat platform made of tree trunks. Two women with long poles walked along the sides, pushing the craft forward against the river's natural flow. As they neared the village, they both pushed toward the opposite bank, propelling the big raft to the shore.

The entire tribe lined the bank of the river as the traders, waved and called out greetings. And there was another surprise as well. Among the sturdy traders, a tall thin figure stood erect. Her regal countenance scanned the riverbank. Jori was the first to notice her.

"Uba-kala! Uba-kala! Look, Devin! Its' Uba-kala!" her gleeful shout caused a stir in the crowd.

Devin looked harder at the crowd. Holding her hand above her eyes to cut the glare, she broke into a grin and trotted toward the place where the "raft" would meet the shore.

"Uba-kala!" Devin echoed Jori's glee. "It IS Uba-kala!"

Devin's friend had finally come to see the village. Devin was thrilled to see her old friend. Uba-kala stepped from the raft to the shore and embraced Devin.

"You have come!" Devin laughed. "You always said it was too far."

"It IS a long journey, my friend." Uba-kala

said serenely. "But traveling on the water is faster than walking. And I had already traveled as far from Solian to the gather land. So when these good women said they were coming up the river, I joined them.

"Have you seen one of these before?" She indicated the raft.

"Oh, my people have seen many bigger ones than this. Ships, they are called. "

Tem shouted for Devin as the trader's leader stepped off the raft.

Devin let go of her friend reluctantly. "I must go and greet the traders in the name of my people. Jori can make you comfortable in my house. I will be with you as soon as I can."

"I understand your duty, my friend. Jori and I have much to talk about. We will see you when you are finished."

Jori stepped forward and greeted Uba-kala warmly. She picked up Uba-kala's pouch and they started toward Devin's house, chatting.

The traders had already lashed the long poles to the corners of the raft sticking the ends deep into the mud of the bank to keep it in place. They were beginning to offload their cargo as Devin approached Tem and the woman to whom she spoke. Tem was laughing merrily.

"Ah, Devin." Tem turned to greet the Queen. "Meet Cee, the leader of the traders' party. Cee, this is our Hunt Queen, Devin."

The little woman smiled up at Devin and touched her heart, making the greeting sign for a friend. "Hello, Devin."

"Hello, Cee." Devin was struck by the look of the woman. She was petite as a child and all her hair was yellow, and floated around her head like a huge flower. Her eyes were the color of new grass. "You are most welcome here. Many have things they wish to trade with your people. We will be glad to have you stay in our visitors' house while you are with us. Come I will show it to you."

Tem and Cee followed Devin to the visitors' house and went inside.

"This is indeed a luxury. We have not slept inside a house for many nights. I thank you for your kindness, Devin." The woman laid her small hand on Devin's bicep. Devin shivered visibly, and little bumps appeared on her tanned forearms. "Perhaps you will join us for a cup of wine later. You could even stay"

"Our cooks will prepare a meal for you." Devin stuttered, taking a step away from the woman. She was a bit flustered by the woman's advance, unsure how to politely refuse.

Tem interceded, her manner polite but businesslike. "Well, I know you have much trading to do today. We will not keep you from your work." And she guided Devin out of the little house and into the sun.

"I will see to the trades, Devin. You must go and greet our other guest."

Devin nodded to the women and walked toward her house.

"So, young leader. I hear you are progressing well in your studies." Uba-kala's warm eyes regarded Jori with amusement.

"You have good ears indeed, if you are hearing about me from all that distance." Jori chuckled.

"I speak to many people." Uba-kala replied. "The traders come to my land too. But they are not the ones who told me about you. Your friend the scout met us coming up the river and had a meal with us."

"Ah. Swain. She has taught me much. My studies will include travels with her. I am looking forward to it."

"You sound restless." Uba-kala lifted one eyebrow expressively.

"A long walk would be good." Jori acknowledged. "But I am in the middle of my training time with the Heschtas. "

"Yes. I am told that you are an exceptional student. That is good. A leader must be educated in many things."

"Here we are." Jori gestured, guiding the woman into Devin's house. "Welcome to Devin's home."

Uba-kala smiled warmly as she entered Devin's hut. She walked slowly around the single room, touching things and smiling. She picked up a little brown statue and turned it over in her hand. The light from the doorway glinted off the elegant carving.

"She treasures that." Jori said quietly. "It was the first thing your family ever made for her. Your youngest daughter, no?"

"Yes. Kmi made it for her at the Gathering. That was the same summer that you helped to teach us the Bear's way to fish, remember?"

Jori remembered that gathering well. She remembered the fishing, and the rituals, and more. "Did you ever hear the story of the trip we had coming home that season?"

"Yes. Tem told me about it. You acted as a scout and ran a whole day to get the Healer. "

"And Kelan led the party home." Jori added.

"Halloo!" Devin called, entering the little house.

She embraced Uba-kala warmly. "So, have you two had a nice talk?"

"Oh, yes." the visitor replied. "We were talking about the Gathering."

"Ah. The planning must be going well if you had time to come and visit us." Devin commented.

"It is going well indeed. But we could use some more help. That is one of the reasons I came. I wanted to see if I could persuade Jori and a few others to come back with me." Uba-kala told her friend.

Jori's heart raced. "Me? You want me? But it is my time with the Heschtas."

Uba-kala grinned.

"We will talk to them." Devin assured her. She turned to the traveler, "But first, I want to show you around the village, and offer you some food and a rest. You have come a long way. "

"Yes. A rest would be good. But not until I see this smoking house of yours."

"That one is my favorite!" Devin laughed. "We finished the stone work on it last fall, along with the walls of the main building. The storage huts will be converted to stone next summer."

A couple of cats darted out as they entered and Ubakala smiled. "Ah. Norahjen's kittens survived then?"

"Oh, yes. There have been several generations of them now. The men's tribe noticed we were keeping cats and even brought us a few new ones from one of their journeys. They do a wonderful job at keeping the vermin from our food storage."

"So first you build with wood and grasses and hay, and then add stone later?" the visitor asked, looking up at the hut's rafters.

"Yes." Devin nodded, "We can build quickly with wood, and then add the stone later."

"And how did you haul all of those rocks here in one season?"

"I made a trade with the men's tribe. They brought us drags of stones and helped to stack them in exchange for smoked fish and cheeses to take on their winter journey. I found out today that they are done working for this season. It is time for their tribe's big hunt and the workers were needed in their own camp."

Jori spent a tense afternoon. Upon her return to the Heschtas house, she was assigned to chop kartof roots into small chunks for dinner. Nita had taught her how to prepare them so they were soft enough for Astaga's old teeth to chew. The pieces were wrapped in wide blades of river grass and were cooked in water until they were soft. They were then laid on a flat surface, and pounded with a stone tool until they were mush. This was tedious work, and did not keep Jori's active mind from worrying about the decision that would be made over dinner.

Tem watched Marjika bartering with one of the traders. Marjika had brought a sack of beads she had made for decorating things. The trader had herbs that Marjika wanted to use for her healing potions. The talk was animated, but friendly.

"Anisa is a good trader." Cee had suddenly appeared by Tem's side.

"So it seems." Tem smiled. "They both seem to be enjoying the negotiation."

"Yes. So, tell me about your Hunt Queen. She seemed nervous in my presence." Cee's soft accent was alluring.

"Devin is normally very confident. But your attention was something she is unused to." Tem told the woman.

"Am I too direct for her? Or has she taken a vow of celibacy?"

"No." Tem chuckled. "She is not a celibate. She and Garnet are mates for life. They do not share pleasure with others. Most people who come here are aware of the pairing and so the issue rarely comes up."

"Ah. A pity. She has strong arms and gentle hands." Cee shrugged. "Do you have a mate for life?"

"I do not." Tem assured her.

The trader Anisa made a signal for Cee to come and approve the final trade. "Duty calls. But we will speak again later."

"We will." Tem said, smiling.

When the time for the meal finally arrived at the Heschtas' house, Jori breathed a sigh of relief. The women would not make her wait until all had eaten before discussing the matter.

"My friend Uba-kala, Hunt Queen of her tribe, has come up the river to visit us and to ask our assistance in the name of the Gather." Devin told them.

"We welcome you, Uba-kala." Nita said politely.

"How can we assist you?" asked Herta.

"One of the women who help with the preparation of the Gather has died. So we are all sad of heart." she paused for a moment and looked truly forlorn. "And," she continued, "She was always accompanied to the Gather by several helpers. They have all stayed in their village to mark her passing."

"You are in need of helpers?" Herta asked.

"We are. And so I have come to you to ask for the assistance of Jori and two others." Uba-kala told the women.

The assent was so immediate and so unanimous that Jori was confused. She shook her head like one of Devin's dogs ridding itself of mud.

"Just like that? I can go?" Jori sputtered.

Devin laughed so hard she fell on the ground. Grinning, Nita answered. "Just like that."

"What about my studies?" Jori demanded.

"Do you propose to spend three moon cycles in my company and learn nothing?" Uba-kala teased.

"It will be good for you to have a mentor from outside our tribe." Herta told the girl, "And to experience the way that the Gathering is organized."

And so it was settled. Jori, Ara, and Riala would go. Ara would work with the builders, Riala with the cooks, and Jori would remain at Uba-kala's side, doing whatever needed to be done.

Having settled the matter, the Heschtas happily turned to other matters. Petrov wanted to know what it was like traveling on the water.

"Well, it is faster." Uba-kala admitted. "But the raft is very small, and you cannot move around much, or it will tip. Also, everyone takes a turn pushing it with the poles, and that it difficult work. If we are to travel back to the gather ground on the water, we must build our own boats. The traders will continue up the river on their route."

"Do you know how?" Devin's eyes lit up at the thought.

"Of course, but there are few of us going, and a raft would be too large to push without a larger party. We will build something else instead."

After the remnants of the meal had been removed, Jori sought out her mother. She found Garnet in the garden, supervising the children, who were thinning out the rows. To Jori's surprise, her mother already seemed to know about the trip.

"You will come to the Gathering this season, will you not?" Jori queried nervously. "After all, the plants grow well, and the women know what to do."

"I will come." Garnet assured her, casually draping one arm over the girl's muscled shoulder. "I have missed it. And I will be missing you, too."

Jori smiled contentedly. "I am excited to go, but afraid too. I have never been on so long a journey without you or Devin."

"You have led parties almost as far." Garnet reminded her.

"But even as I led, I always knew you were there. " Jori mused.

"You are ready." Garnet's voice was full of confidence. But her eyes were full of something else.

"If you are sure, then why are you sad, mother?" Jori pulled the woman into her arms for a hug.

"You have grown so tall!" Garnet laughed, hugging her back. "I am not sad, Jori, only proud. You are smart and strong, and will be a great help to Uba-kala this season. Now go and make your preparations. I will come to the Heschtas' house tonight to sit with you by the fire."

Later, as she sat sharpening her arrows, Jori put voice to her puzzlement. "Herta, why was my mother sad? She said she was proud, but her eyes filled."

"There comes a day for every mother when she realizes that her child has grown, and will start a new life. It is a good day, and a happy one, but bittersweet; for it means that the child will no longer be in your care." Herta told the girl. "Being a mother is a paradox. The ultimate job of any parent is to make yourself unneeded by your child. The day that your child leaves you to make her own life is the day you have completed your task. On that day, you will feel happy that you have done a good job, proud of your child's growth, and sadness too. I think your mother saw that moment today."

Jori was silent for a while. The only sound was the arrow point rubbing on the big stone.

"They have both been wonderful parents." Jori commented.

"Yes, they have." Herta agreed. "You have been lucky. And now is the time to show them your gratitude."

"How?"

"By doing a good job and being a good leader."

After the next sun rose, Uba-kala walked with Ara and Jori and Riala into the woods. She pointed out two large fallen tree trunks that they would need to build the 'boats'. She instructed the girls to go and get help to drag the trunks to a spot near the new visitor's house on the bank of the river.

When the girls trotted away in search of extra muscle, she returned to the village in search of Devin.

Devin was walking back from the traveler's house, having said goodbye to the traders.

"Ah, my friend. There you are." Devin greeted her.

"I have put my new apprentices to work." Uba-kala pointed in the direction the girls had gone. "They are bringing tree trunks for the boats."

Devin looked in the direction indicated. "Good. So tell me, how does one turn a tree into a boat?"

"You have no doubt seen dead tree trunks floating down the river." Uba-kala said.

"Well, of course." Devin acknowledged.

"All we must do then is to hollow out the top side of the log so we have a place to sit. We can use long paddles to push the boat where we want it to go."

"Ahh." Devin nodded, understanding. "Your people are very smart, my friend!"

"As are yours. It will take the girls all morning to get the logs to the river. While they are working, would you show me your storage houses? I wish to see all that you have built here. And I want another look at the smoke-house. I have questions."

The old friends walked over to the smoke house, and Devin explained.

"Your people dry meats to preserve them, do you not?"

"Of course." Uba-kala told her. "And we use the salt we get from you to help the wind do its work."

"We do the same. But we have found that if we keep a smoky fire going while the meat dries, it absorbs a good flavor."

They entered the smoke house, and Devin pointed up. "We hang the meat up in the rafters. I made special pegs up there. See?"

"I do." said Uba-kala, smiling. "So the smoke takes the place of the wind."

"Yes. Your people enlist the help of the wind to dry your meats. We enlist the fire."

"And if the meat dries inside this house, it is protected from predators." Uba-kala reasoned.

"In the winter we sometimes get a curious bear or cat." Devin said, "When their hunting is scarce and they smell the meat. But they have to be very hungry to come so near so many humans."

Uba-kala nodded, still looking at the bundles that hung above her head. "And fish too? And fowl!"

"Whatever we have. We also make cheese and smoke it this way, in the fruit house. "

"That is a wonderful food, and strange. Tell me how it is made again?"

"Well, we start with milk from goats. We trade the milk with the men's tribe for smoked fish or boar. Then Wren makes the milk into a soft cheese, like the food you call Feta. We add different herbs than you, and then we wrap it in thin hides and hang it up, like the meat. When spring comes, it is ready. I will send some along with you on your journey."

They walked across the compound toward the great hearth fire and sat on the low wall. Devin seemed suddenly pensive.

"What troubles you, friend?" Uba-kala was genuinely concerned.

"I have still not brought water to the village, even though I have drawings of your system."

Uba-kala laughed explosively. "Why would you take the trouble to build pathways for the water when you have so much all around you?"

Devin looked up, startled.

"We were forced to build that system because in our land, there is little water and it must be shared by many." Uba-kala told her. "In my lands, you can dig and dig for an entire cycle of the moon and never hit water. Here, you are surrounded by water. If I lived in this land, I would simply dig a hole and line it with bricks."

"The water is under the ground???" Devin asked excitedly.

"Yes, my friend. My ancestors had no rivers or streams to take water from, but still they noticed that some plants grew in certain places. They could not drink the salty water of the sea. So, they reasoned that those plants must have been getting water from under the ground. They dug and dug, and finally found a stream bubbling up. To this day that stream is the source of water for our entire village."

"So you build the pathways to bring the water into your village." Devin's blue eyes lit up, finally understanding.

"Yes." Uba-kala confirmed. "But this, you do not have to do."

Ara fell with a thump. Startled, she looked around herself.

"Are you all right?" Jori started around the tree to assist her.

She waved Jori back to her position and got to her feet. "I think I tripped over that root. Nothing hurt but my pride."

Jori looked her over, smiling. "Let me take the front for a while. You take the other end so you can walk facing forward."

They traded places and resumed dragging the tree toward the water's edge. Of course, it was not walking backward that had made Ara trip. She had done that a hundred times. She had simply not been paying attention. She was too busy gazing at Jori's muscled shoulders to see where her feet were going. The day was sunny and hot, and the sweat glistened on Jori's tanned skin. Ara was captivated. She smiled, thinking of the many long nights that they would share over the summer while they were away from the village.

Riala approached, running. "I can help too," she said, taking up a position and starting to pull.

"Oh, thanks, Riala." Jori smiled. "That makes it easier."

They reached the water's grassy bank and left the tree next to the other one that they had already brought.

"Anyone for a swim?" Ara grinned. "I need to cool off." She leapt into the cool water, making a big splash without waiting for an answer.

Jori and Riala followed, laughing. The girls splashed and dove in the cool water, chasing and dunking one another until their noise attracted the attention of Uba-kala and Devin.

"Good. You have brought the trees." Uba-kala praised them, ignoring their silliness. "And as soon as you are refreshed, I will show you how to begin the work."

Even with Daña, Tem and a few of the Heschtas coming by to help, it took two full days to chip away all the wood from the interior section, and another full day to make the front end come to a point. Ubakala said they must be pointed on the front to help them glide through the water with less work.

Once they had completed those tasks, they turned their attention to gathering branches with which to make paddles. While the women whittled, Uba-kala had explained how, in her homeland, that some women used fire to hollow out the trunks to make canoes. It took a full day to make the paddles, and the women passed the time by telling stories or singing songs as they worked.

When Uba-kala was finally satisfied with the result, she took the girls out one at a time to show them how to maneuver the little crafts. Many of the women from the village came to watch this part of the process. They applauded when the first canoe was pushed into the water by Ara, and laughed as each of the girls tipped the boat and fell in. Uba-kala took the wettings good naturedly, saying that it was a normal part of the learning. One of Devin's dogs jumped into one canoe, and stood with his front feet on the edge, wagging his tail.

Of course, Devin, Tem and Garnet would not be left out; each of them in turn was taught by the girls how to manage the little boats. The women on the shore found this part quite amusing. Devin landed in the water several times. Tem got the boat stuck on a beaver dam. Three of the women from the village had to wade out and help push them off.

Garnet, however, seemed to have an instinct for it. From the moment she got into the canoe with Riala her boat glided effortlessly. As she landed the boat to the cheers of the women, Jori approached.

"Well done mother!" Jori exclaimed, wading in alongside them. "But you are the only one who has not had a swim yet." And grinning, she tipped the canoe.

Spring, 1986 C.E.

I sat on the swing, smoking one of the little vanilla cigars I had come to enjoy, watching the ritual preparations. The old woman was hobbling around the yard, hiding small items, like boiled eggs and carrots in crooks of trees and under the porch and other places. She said she was leaving the gifts of spring out for the spirits. I smiled, remembering the easter egg hunts of my youth.

After a while, she came and plopped down next to me. She sat still, watching me enjoying my cigar. I had become used to her scrutiny, so I simply continued to look around the yard and smoke. I knew she would come out with whatever it was she wanted to say eventually.

"It is time for the ritual." She said.

"Ritual? What ritual?" I asked.

She tilted her head. Her expression was a war between pity and annoyance.

She pointed up. "You see the sun? You see where it is in sky? You know what it means when sun is in that direction?"

"Spring is here." I said.

"Yes. We have survived the winter. We must offer gifts of gratitude, and break first ground. Here." She handed me a short wooden stick with one pointed end and one flat end. It was gray with age.

Since I had watched her hide the offerings, I assumed I was to break ground for her. I took the stick and looked at it.

"This is very old." She said. "Very old...what you call...shovel... A Special spring shovel. The Pointy end to get through grass... Flat end to move dirt. It has magic to bring a good growing season. Be careful with it. Dig small hole." She rose and indicated where she wanted her hole.

I sighed and followed, dropping to my knees and trying to use the "shovel" to dig. It was harder work than it would have been with a modern tool. The handle of the shovel had carvings of rabbits. It felt warm in my hand. I could almost feel the hands of my ancestors covering and guiding my own.

When the hole was wide and deep as she wanted it, Aranna pulled a small doll out of her skirts. It was a primitive figure, made of grasses and wrapped in a scrap of cloth that resembled a sari. She unwrapped the figure to reveal seeds tucked into the middle. She carefully pulled out three seeds and handed them to me, and then lovingly re-wrapped the doll, kissed its forehead and tucked it away again. She held out her hand for the seeds.

She carefully placed the seeds in the hole I had dug, patting the loose dirt around them. She spoke a few words in a language I did not recognize. She spent a few moments in silence, looking down at the new planting.

"We do this for a good growing season." She said to me. You do this every Spring from now on, just like your people. She sat up and looked me straight in the eyes. "I give you this tool. Use it for this ritual only. Keep it safe for the women to come."

I blinked back inexplicable tears. A big strong Dyke like me shouldn't cry over a stick. But somehow this moment meant something bigger. I was becoming the Rememberer. My heart was so full I could barely breathe. She was passing the torch to me. I smiled, thinking of something eloquent to say.

She interrupted my moment, saying. "Now you go and dig up the rest of the garden. I will finish planting tomorrow. Now I rest." She got up and hobbled toward the house.

I took the stick and put it carefully away, next to my personal things near my bed. As I turned to go back outside, I heard her shrill voice. "Back to work, young one! You have no time for a nap today."

Being The Rememberer is not all glamour and autograph signing, I thought sullenly, The Hearth Queen still gives you chores.

Summer, 3778 B.C.E.

The air was chill on Jori's arms as the little group slid silently across the water. In the shadowy light of dawn, they could see animals along the banks that had come to drink or fish. There was silence on the river, except for the quiet lapping of the paddles as the party progressed. Jori smiled, watching Ara's shoulders move in rhythm to her own as she sat in the front of the canoe. She filled her lungs with cool, clear air and exhaled slowly. She made a silent prayer to The Mother, 'Thank you mother, for the beautiful river and the beautiful morning, and most of all for the beautiful Ara.' As though she had heard, Ara turned and smiled.

They had been traveling for several days now, stopping each day for a rest and a meal when the sun was its hottest, and then traveling again until the sun began to set. At some places the water was almost even with the riverbank. In those sections the party could see across the sweeping landscape. In other places, like this one, the bank was higher, and trees lined the river, making a sort of enclosed space. Like a room made of trees, Jori thought, smiling.

Suddenly the other canoe veered toward a low spot on the shore. Jori followed, wondering why. As she pulled alongside, Riala jumped out and pulled the canoe up on the bank. Ara turned to look at Jori questioningly. Jori shrugged, and Ara jumped out of the canoe to beach it.

When they all stood on the grassy bank, Uba-kala explained. "Just a little way down the river, there are rapid waters. And even though you are all doing well in your boats, you will need to be well rested for that. We will camp early tonight, and I will instruct you. Come, we will walk down river a little so I can show you what I mean."

Soon, the girls could see what Uba-kala meant. There was a place where the river narrowed, ran over some big rocks, and was turbulent. The current veered and turned this way and that around and among the rocks and the natural dams. Jori remarked that it would indeed take great skill to navigate one of the little canoes through the rapid waters. Uba-kala explained that there were also currents that ran under the water as well. She told them that these undercurrents were erratic, and probably more of a danger than the rocks themselves. She pointed to the places on the water where the channel looked deepest.

"You see that flat water that winds around and through the rocks? You should try to follow it. The current there is fast, but where the surface is flat, there are no rocks near enough to the surface to harm the boat." She told them. Fortunately, this section is not very long, and so a good one to learn on. Later in the trip, there are larger sections to be dealt with." Riala looked worried. Uba-kala threw a companionable arm around the girl's shoulder. "Do not worry, little one. You are doing well. And I have faith in you."

They returned to the place where they had left the canoes, and began to set up their little camp. Ara went off to find wood for a fire. Riala and Jori laid out the sleeping rolls.

"How many more days to the Gather ground?" Riala asked.

"Do you not enjoy our journey?" Uba-kala teased.

"Yes, but every journey must come to an end. When will this one do so?" she smirked up at the leader.

Uba-kala chuckled, and slapped her own knee. "You are a quick one, Riala! We will be there in four or five more sleeps."

"And will we meet more of your people there?"

"You mean people from my village? Oh, yes. There are a few. And many more women from many other places, too."

"How do they all talk to each other? Do they all speak our language, like you?" Ara asked the woman.

"Oh, no, young one. They all speak

differently. "She explained. "Still, we have managed to communicate all of these years. Some speak more than their own languages, and that can be helpful."

Ara looked puzzled, so Uba-kala went on. "Do you not communicate with Devin's dogs? They have no words at all. But still they seem to understand what you want them to do, no?"

"Well, yes." Ara said haltingly.

"And women are much smarter than dogs, are they not?" she asked the girl.

"Yes, of course."

"So, we find a way." Uba-kala smiled at the girls and leaned back against a tree, closing her eyes to nap. "We rest now for a little while." As though that ended the matter, Uba-kala fell instantly asleep.

Ara moved close, laying her head on Jori's shoulder. She sighed, smiling. This was the place in the world that she most loved: lying alongside Jori and touching. Jori's big forearm wound around her, and the strong hands slowly traveled in circles on her back. She slid her hand around the back of Jori's head and pulled her face down for a kiss.

"We should sleep, love." Jori whispered, squeezing her close. "Tomorrow will be a long day."

"Yes. We should." Ara smiled, looking up into her eyes.

But they didn't.

~~~~

Swain trotted toward the men. One waved, smiling. Toban, she thought, and Dain? It was unusual to see the old man out of the village these days. Usually he would simply send Toban, as his apprentice to look for plants for his potions.

She had been down river, following Uba-kala's party for two sleeps. She had accompanied Norahjen, who was trailing behind the party to keep watch on the girls. Norahjen was on her way to the gathering too, but didn't want to inhibit the girls' independent first journey by joining them. And after a lifetime of being a scout, she had come to prefer the solitude of traveling alone.

Swain had accompanied her for a time, turning back to the village to carry the message that they were well on their way. As she crossed the grassy flats on her return run, she had noticed a few specs in the distance, and had turned toward them to see what animal or human grazed here. She ran toward the figures, realizing soon that it was her friend Toban and another, older man. She trotted up to them, making the hand signal for friend.

"Greetings, friends." She said, smiling.

"Swain." Toban grinned at her. "How are you?"

"I am well, thank you Toban." she replied. And, turning to the old healer she said loudly. "Greetings, healer. I am glad the sun finds you well and strong."

The old man nodded, smiling up at the scout.

"We are gathering herbs." he said.

"So I have seen," she told him, nodding. "I was on the way back to the village when I saw you."

"So, the journey begins well?" Toban asked.

"You are well informed, my friend." Swain said, impressed. "Yes. They are progressing quickly downstream. I had to run to keep up for part of the way. Those boats can move very fast."

"So I have heard." Toban laughed with her.

"I have some rabbits that I trapped yesterday. Will you stop and share a meal?" she asked the men.

Toban looked at the old healer, who nodded gratefully. "We will." He told Swain.

Toban made a good place for the old man to rest and got him settled as Swain gathered fuel and started a small cooking fire. Soon the juices from the meat were spitting and sputtering, and their lunch was beginning to smell succulent.

Toban and Swain squatted facing one another, the fire between them.

"So, Toban," She started, "How are things in your tribe these days? We have not heard from Falcone all summer."

"He is progressing well. He has recovered his speech, and he can walk. He still moves stiffly and slowly, though." Toban told her.

She turned to compliment Dain on his healing skills, but he was snoring softly, his head nodding forward. They smiled at one another indulgently. The man was a great healer, but he was getting very old. Swain expressed her surprise at seeing him here, gathering herbs himself.

"Why has he come?" she whispered. "Does he not let you gather plants for him?"

"He does. But there is one potion whose recipe he has kept from me all this time. The final lesson, he says." Toban told her.

"So once he shows it to you, then you are the healer?" she asked.

"Well, there is much ceremony, but yes. Essentially that is true." Toban said. "Of course I cannot tell you about the rituals."

"Of course" Swain knew that he could not divulge the secrets of his camp, even to a close friend. She was unoffended. There were many things she would not tell him, either.

"And how are things in your village?" he asked. "Is my mother well?"

"Of course. All is well. They have all been making boats and playing in them." She told him, grinning. "Your mother, in particular seems to have the knack."

They ate companionably, chatting about the small happenings in the villages. When it was time to leave, Swain hugged her friend and asked, "Will your tribe make a visit this summer to the village?"

Shaking his head sadly, he replied, "I do not think so. Falcone still reacts with anger whenever someone mentions it: Though I know that a few have visited secretly."

"Yes." she smiled. "I have seen Lexis coming

and going. He says he likes to visit Marjika and the children. But why is Falcone so angry?"

"His pride is hurt. To be rescued by Devin has injured it. His mood will change. But for now, he struts around talking about how he needs no woman for anything." Toban shook his head, chuckling.

"I do not understand it. He was trapped because he made bad decisions. We only helped." Swain was puzzled.

"Yes. It was his fault that we became trapped. I think that is part of the problem. He is embarrassed to have needed rescue. As for the hatred of the women, I do not understand, either."

"He looks at the world through different eyes than yours or mine." Old Dain's voice startled them. They had thought him asleep. "He was not born of this tribe, you know."

"I had heard that he had been a foundling, brought to the village by Norahjen." Toban acknowledged. "But he lived at Z's fire and was taught as all of our children are until he was old enough to go with the men."

Z was the grandmother of both Toban and Jori, and Garnet's mother. She was Hearth Queen before Garnet. Her name whole name was Zuszansuskhanna. Most of the tribe except for Norahjen called her Zuzu, or simply Z. Norahjen, with whom she was romantically involved, called her "Hannah".

"Yes. He was found by Norahjen. But that is

not the whole story, Toban. He had seen six or seven winters with the tribe of his birth. They cast him out, because he was small and clumsy. They called him a 'runt'. And while he was taken in and cared for by our people, he was with his original tribe long enough to absorb much or their culture."

"What tribe would cast out a child? Even a sickly or small one?" Swain was incredulous. The idea was so foreign that she could almost not comprehend it.

"They are called the Gols. They are a wandering tribe that lives by attacking small groups and taking their things. They so not look to the Mother. Rather, they cite a male deity they call 'God'. They think of women as lesser beings than men. They value only strength and speed. Falcone was a son of a leader. But he was small and not strong. So they left him to die in the mountains." Swain and Toban brimmed with questions, but Dain's story had worn him out, and his head sank again to his chest.

"I had heard a legend of a tribe like that, who attacked other tribes, burned their camps and stole their possessions. I had heard that they force certain women to go with them. They call them 'wives'. I think it is the word in their language for slaves." Toban told her.

She sat back, absorbing the story. "Surely this is simply a story told to scare children into behaving well, is it not?"

"I wish it were. We have met up with bands

of these Gols on our travels. They tend to leave us be, as we have nothing they value. But I would not like to think of any young child staying with them. I did not know that my father was born of them." Toban shook his head sadly. "Perhaps the blow to Falcone's head shook out some of his early teaching. That would explain the odd things he has been saying...." Toban lapsed into thoughtful silence, staring into the flames.

"Well, as you say, as he heals, this episode may pass. " Swain rose and dusted off her leggings. "I would like to be home before darkness comes, so I will take my leave now. I hope to see you again soon, my friend." she said.

"I hope so too. Please give my greetings to my mother and Devin for me. Tell them that I am well and will visit when I can." He stood, and clutched forearms with her in a sign of affection.

"I will," she waved as she strode off toward the village.

She was puzzled by the story Dain had told, by the things Toban had said about his tribe, and by what he hadn't said.

Lexis had mentioned Falcone's hatred of the women too. And that Falcone had vowed never to return to the village. Falcone had raged on, Lexis had told her, saying that there were many villages with women who he could visit: Women who would not challenge his authority.

He was getting crazy in his old age, just as Shayana had in her final seasons. She sent a wish to the mother for the safety and health of her friends' tribe.

Upon her return to the village, she reported to the Heschtas' house, where she found Devin sitting near the fire with Astaga.

"So, Swain." Devin asked after the ritual greetings had been exchanged, "How is the party progressing?"

"Quickly!" Swain told her friend. "Those boats move very fast. They seem to be well on their way. And Norahjen will be nearby in case of trouble."

"Good. I will tell Garnet to stop worrying about them." Devin said.

"Do you think she will?" Astaga asked, her dark eyes had an amused glint.

"Of course not. But I will tell her. Having Norahjen behind them will help to comfort her." Devin smiled. "Will you stay tonight?"

"I will stay for a day or two. I need to make some arrows. And a comfortable night or two will be welcome." Swain told her friend.

"Good. I have not had a game of bones since last winter." Devin said. "We can get Daña and Tem to play too, if you desire it."

"You wish to try again to win against me?" Swain asked, smirking. The last time they had played the game, Swain had won many rounds, and many bets.

Devin's eyes glinted with amusement. "I wish to see you try to win against ME."

"We shall see." Swain grinned. "First I want a washing and a long nap." Her face turned serious. "But before I go to the river, I have something else to report."

Devin leaned forward, sensing the change in mood. "What is it?"

"I saw Toban and Dain in the field, gathering herbs." she said. "Toban sent his regards to you and to his mother. And he spoke of the mood in his camp."

"Does his description match Lexis'?" Astaga asked.

"Yes. He is very careful about what he can reveal. But he does say that Falcone is acting strangely." Swain explained. "That he is making comments about you and our tribe. Apparently, though, everyone there does not agree with him."

"But he is their leader until he dies or stands down. You know how it works for them. They do not look upon him in the same way our tribe looks upon me, or Garnet. The men's tribe seems to serve their leader. In our tribe, the leader serves the people. " Devin mused. "His tribe will follow him, even if they feel he is wrong. Still, Lexis comes to visit, and a few others."

"But quietly. Toban says that they sneak out of their camp." Swain explained. "They fear Falcone's temper if he found them coming here."

"I do not understand why anyone, leader or not, would try to influence the reason of another." Devin sighed. "For all that I know about the men's tribe, I do not understand their hearts."

"Yes. I feel the same. I cannot comprehend why one person would want to control the thoughts of another. But Falcone seems to think that his role as leader entitles him to that. It is as though he possesses his tribe instead of serving it." Swain was shaking her head sadly. "Old Dain told us the story of how Falcone came to be in our tribe. Do you know it?"

"I do. Falcone has risen above much adversity to get to a position of leadership. I can only hope that his strength of will reasserts itself and his reason returns with his physical health. As for his tribe," Devin said, standing, "It is not for us to decide how they should live. We can only trust the Mother that all will be well with them and us. And I am keeping you from your swim." She patted Swain's shoulder and walked toward the center of the village.

Swain watched her go, pondering the differences between the tribes. She was glad to live among these good women. Digging in her pack, she found the soapy root she sought. She stood; removing her garments, and strode toward the river.

~~~~

The nose of the little canoe bounced. Ara leaned forward to counter the motion as   Jori moved the paddle in an arc to bring them back around. Their direction corrected, they continued to glide quickly over the water. Ara's breath caught as a large boulder loomed ahead and then as quickly slid past them on her right. She could barely hear Jori shouting commands over the rush of water. Seeing another rock on the left and much too close, she swung her paddle over and pushed at it. The boat veered. As they came alongside, Jori pushed on the rock as well. They made a good team, instinctively supporting or countering one another's moves.

Ara grinned. She felt so alive! Her heart pounded loudly, and it seemed that all of her senses were heightened. She grinned as she manipulated the paddle in response to Jori's signals.

The rapids seemed to last only a few minutes. But when they finally reached smooth water again, the sun was beginning to descend. Jori looked around for the other boat, which had been behind them at the beginning of the day. Within seconds, the other craft appeared. Riala looked a little ashen, but Uba-kala was smiling. She made a hand sign for them to make their way to the first low spot on shore, and Jori led the party to the landing.

"That was fun!" Ara called out to the woman as they dragged the boats up the bank for the night.

Uba-kala grinned at the girl. "You all did very well."

Seeing Riala's face, Ara added. "There were some pretty scary moments, though. I thought that big rock would hit us."

Riala made no comment.

Jori and Riala began to make a fire. They

would need to get their clothes dry, and cook some food. Everyone's feet were wet up to the knees. Ara helped Uba-kala bring their bundles up to the spot they had chosen for sleep. They were all tired from their exertions.

Once they had eaten and laid their wet garments on rocks near the fire to dry, they sat chatting about their experience until the light was well gone.

"So how do you all feel?" Uba-kala asked the girls.

"I am full of energy!" Ara told the woman. "I could run to the gather ground this night."

"The excitement affects many in that way. But you will need your rest. So I will Prepare a calming tea to help you sleep."

When the tea was read, Ara took a drink of the liquid and squinted. "Odd taste. What is it?"

"Some herbs from my people. They different than yours. We add dates." The woman explained.

Riala refused her cup at first, saying she was tired enough to sleep.

"Oh, your body is tired all right. But the rapids are frightening as well as exciting, and I want your mind to rest too." Uba-kala told her. "So drink."

"This drink makes my belly warm." Jori commented. "It would be good for the winters at home. Perhaps I will trade for some when we reach the gather to help me stay warm in the snow."

"These herbs are rare an precious in our land, and used only for ritual or medicine." Uba-kala told her.

Finally, Uba-kala sent them off to their beds, saying that they had only two or three more days' travel to the gather ground. Riala's body was tired, but as her mentor had suggested, her mind was still spinning. She took a few calming breaths, willing herself to relax. She concentrated on the warmth that was spreading outward from her stomach, and held the image of her home village in her mind. Comforted, she drifted off to sleep.

That same night in the village, some of the Heschtas were taking some time to relax as well. The light from the fire glinted off Astaga's craggy features as she inhaled the smoke from the pipe. She held it in for a moment, passing the pipe on to Tem.

"Thanks for bringing the herbs, Astaga. Is this the last of your trade?" Tem asked. Astaga had received these herbs at the gather ground the previous summer from a member of another tribe. She had been accompanying Wren while she traded salt for curry and other spices. While Wren bargained, Astaga had noticed a very beautiful woman inhaling the smoke from a pipe. The aroma was very sweet, and she approached the woman and asked about it.

Astaga smiled, remembering the long and very enjoyable afternoon she had spent with the woman. She had gained more than herbs in trade on that day. "Yes. This is the last of it. Perhaps I will see her again this summer." Astaga said as she exhaled. "My turn." She took the flat bone pieces from Petrov and shook them in her hands. She tossed them down and smiled. "Two Water and a blank. That makes three. That ties you, Devin." She passed the little stones on to Tem.

Tem took them, grinning. She held the bones, cupped inside her hands, up to her forehead for a moment. Then she tossed them. "There! A cycle! I win!"

The participants groaned. Devin slapped the earth with her palm. Tem had thrown one of each symbol. That was an automatic win. The set consisted of two tiles of each symbols for Earth, Fire, Water, Air, Mother and blank. The blank represented luck and so could be used for anything.

"How does she DO that?" Astaga asked, exasperated. They had been playing this game since they were children. Tem had always been good at it. It seemed to her that Tem was even better at it when they were wagering.

Grinning, Tem gathered up the little pile of things they had bet. "Not bad." she said. "This is a nice knife sheath, Petrov."

Petrov, who was just inhaling smoke, nodded. "Well, we do not often play for bets, so I brought something good."

"Where is Swain?" Astaga asked.

"She had…something else to do before she came here." Devin grinned. "She has been alone a long time."

"Oh? Visiting a woman, is she?" Astaga smiled. "Good. She has been too long away from the village." Leaning forward conspiratorially, she asked, "Who is it?"

"Anna." Tem said. "They went for a walk up river this afternoon and haven't come back yet."

"Anna? Nice." Devin said appreciatively, inhaling deeply.

Petrov looked puzzled. "Should we go and look for them? Maybe they are lost."

They all laughed. "No, friend." Astaga explained. "They are just enjoying their time alone. Swain will be along soon."

"But what if…oh." They all saw the idea dawn on Petrov, and laughed harder. The usually quick-witted drummer laughed at herself too. "This herb has me fuzzy. Well—good for Swain!"

"What is good for me?" Swain's voice came through the doorway of the little hut. Her lanky body followed it, and squinted. "It looks like you have thrown wet leaves on the fire in here. And smells like…hey-give me some!" She reached for the pipe.

"Astaga was asking where you were." Tem explained.

"The land of dreams." Swain grinned between puffs.

"I hope you did not leave her company for ours." Petrov said.

Swain shook her head vigorously, making negative grunts as she held her breath.

"If you had, I would wonder about your sanity." Devin laughed.

Exhaling loudly, Swain said, "I would never do that! Anna is too much fun to be with, and too pretty. She had to look in on someone. Perhaps I will visit her house again later."

"She is a good healer. Her manner is very comforting." Devin said, eyes twinkling

"I would never sacrifice time with her to play bones with you, even if I DO always win." Swain chuckled.

"You will not win this night!" Tem laughed. "Let's play another round."

"It is my turn to go first." Astaga said, picking up the bones. "Lay down your risk."

Across the village, the scene was much more subdued. "Rest easily. Marianna. This injury will heal and you will be swimming again soon. But you must sleep now." Anna was telling the girl, whose big dark eyes looked at her fearfully. She had given the girl something ease the pain and lower her anxiety. In these cases, sleep was best. It gave the injury time to heal.

She tucked the furs up around the girl's chin and smiled reassuringly. The brown eyes closed and the child sighed. Anna retreated quietly from the darkened house.

Daña stood talking with Garnet in hushed tones.

"She has been restless, Anna." Daña told her. "I have been having trouble keeping her in her bed."

"You have done well for her, my friend. Tomorrow she can go outside for a short walk. It will be good to begin exercising that leg as soon as possible." Anna said.

"Remember when Devin broke her leg? She was the same as your daughter, Daña. Always wanting to push herself further than she should." Garnet added.

"Thank you for your attention, Anna." Daña hugged her friends, "and your comfort, Garnet. I was pretty scared for her."

"It is always serious when one breaks a bone. But this one did not puncture the skin, and seems to be holding in place with the hide strips. "Daña assured her.

"Devin's leg has healed completely." Garnet said, patting her shoulder. "It will be well."

"Perhaps Kelan will come and be with her tomorrow." Daña said hopefully. "Marianna has always loved her so!"

"I will speak to Kelan." Garnet told them. "I am sure she will want to help. She has always loved Marianna, too."

Anna hugged the woman warmly "Now stop worrying and go and sleep. You have made yourself overtired with worry. You cannot tend her if you are exhausted."

The women quietly retreated outside, leaving Dana and the girl to rest.

"Well, Anna, our duty is done. Will you go and seek Swain?" Garnet asked, grinning.

"No. She is at the Heschtas hut with the rest of them, playing bones. She will return to my house when they are finished." Anna answered.

"I am glad to see you relaxing together." Garnet told her.

The two friends walked leisurely to Garnet's house and sat down on the stools Devin had made just outside Garnet's door.

"I was very glad to see her. She has been away so much this spring." Anna told her. "It has been a long time since she has stayed in the village."

"Yes, we have kept her busy." Garnet commented.

"How does the girls' trip down the river go?"

"Swain said that it goes well. They apparently have the knack of the little boats." Garnet told her. "And Uba-kala has my trust, and Devin's."

"But you have worried about them nonetheless, no?" Anna's gaze scrutinized the leader's face.

"Yes. But that is the way with children, is it not?" Garnet laughed. "You trust them, and yet you worry; A paradox."

"So should we go and join the game after all?" Anna tilted her chin in the direction of the Heschtas' hut.

"No. I dislike the smell of that herb they are using. And my presence there may inhibit them."

Garnet said. "I am happy to sit here and look at the stars with you, my friend. Devin will be along when they are done."

"True enough." Anna said, "I dislike the smell of that herb too."

It was late into the night before the game finally ended. Swain had indeed won a few rounds. But Tem had won a few as well. The women said good night to the inhabitants of the house, and walked unsteadily out into the night, laughing. Tem noticed that Swain was leaving with them.

"Will you not sleep here?" Tem asked.

"Not if Anna will welcome my presence." Swain told her friend. "I will go and see if she is awake."

"If Garnet is asleep I will awaken her." Devin told them. Her speech was a little slow, and she grinned drunkenly.

"I will be off, then." Tem told her friends and disappeared into the night.

"Where is she going?" Swain asked. "Her house is over there." She pointed in the opposite direction.

"Tem never explains." Devin said complacently. She knew whose house was in the direction that her best friend had gone. But Barde and Tem did not choose to speak of their attachment. So while Devin knew all about it, she would respect their privacy.

"Well, I am off to see the beautiful Anna." Swain said, waving goodbye.

"Good night, friend." Devin called after her. She turned in the direction of Garnet's house, smiling.

~~~~

The little band of travelers was on the water as the sun rose the next morning.

Uba-kala had given Riala and Ara long strings with large thorns ties to the ends. On these thorns, she impaled fat worms. She instructed the two girls to leave the thorns in the water and hold the other end of the line so that the worms seemed to "swim" through the water as the canoes moved. The end of the line the girls held was wound around a stick. Uba-kala told the girls that fishes would see the worms as food. She said that when the fish bit onto the worms, they would be snagged by the thorns and the girls could pull them into the canoes.

She cautioned the party that this technique only worked when they were moving through slow deep water. When they were moving through shallow or rough water, the thorns would become snagged on logs and debris lying under the surface. But this day's section of the river was calm and deep, and so they could be hunting and travelling at the same time.

The sun shone warmly on the surface of the river, and Jori had a pleasant day, paddling along and looking at the riverbanks and the sky. At intervals, they would stop so the girls could pull in and check the lines and "bait" (as Uba-kala told them it was called). Several times, when the girls pulled the string in there had been fish wriggling on the end! Uba-kala showed them how to remove the fish from the thorn, store it in a sack that hung from the gunnel. She said that keeping the sack submerged in the water would keep the fish fresh for an entire day until they could make camp that afternoon.

Ara was thrilled! She had caught three fish for dinner. Riala had also caught two fish. It was enough to make a merry meal. They came around a bend in the river and found a camping place. On one side was a low sandy beach that led gently to the foot of a tall hill. On the other was a steep cliff.

Suddenly, Ara pointed and shouted "LOOK!" She pointed toward a lone figure standing on the hill above the bank ahead. The sun was setting behind the woman, creating a reddish aura around her. She was tall and brown, like Uba-kala. And she was waving. Jori turned her head to look at the other boat. Yes, Uba-kala had seen. She was waiving too, and heading for the bank below where the woman stood.

When they beached the canoes, Uba-kala ran up the bank and embraced the woman, laughing. They talked very fast in a language that the girls had heard but did not understand.

"This is my mate, Ashe." Uba-kala told them, grinning. "She is scout for the gathering."

Jori touched her palm to her heart in the

traditional greeting of friends. "Hello. I am Jori, daughter of Garnet."

Ashe smiled warmly. "Yes. Jori. I know your mother. And I have hunted with Devin."

"And this is Ara, and Riala." Jori indicated her friends. The two girls also made the greeting symbol, smiling.

"Are we close to the gather ground, Ashe?" Riala asked.

Uba-kala laughed, "She has been anxious to arrive ever since we left her village. I do not think that Riala likes the boats very much."

Riala looked stricken. "But- "

"It's all right, child." Uba-kala assured her, patting her shoulder. "You have done very well. But I have sensed your restlessness."

"We are not far now from the encampment." Ashe told the girls. "And I do not prefer to travel on the water either, Riala. I would rather travel on my own good legs."

"I do love to travel." Riala said "But you are right. I would rather walk than ride in a boat."

"Come now, let's cook those lovely fish you have caught, and take our rest. We can make for the encampment in the morning."

The encampment turned out to be five or six hide tents in a semi-circle. Jori stood, her mouth open, staring. She had never seen this site with so few inhabitants before. It was as though an entire village had vanished.

"But where is the hearth? And the dance ground? Where is the big eating tent?" Ara sputtered.

Uba-kala's merry laugh lit the sky. "They have not been put up yet. So now you see why we needed your help. There is much work to do before the sisters arrive. "

"We build the encampment anew each time? Why not just leave it up?" Riala seemed perplexed.

"For several reasons;" Ashe explained. "One reason is that there is no one here during the winter to take care of things. A big storm or an elk herd could destroy all of the big tents and no one would know. Then when we arrived in the spring, we would have to create them all again. What we do is take down everything and store it. This way it is preserved for the next season."

"And the most important reason is that we all believe that we should leave this place as the Mother made it when we are not using it. We are from many tribes and have many beliefs. But one of the things upon which we all agree is this: we should use the gifts of the Mother wisely. We use what we need, but only what we need. "

Riala smiled up at the tall scout. "So when do we begin?"

"Not this day, child. This day we will raise a tent for you girls. You need to rest after your long trek. Or at least I need to." Uba-kala told them. "Today you will meet everyone and this evening we will have a talk around the fire about what plans the group has agreed upon."

~~~~

"Help! Devin! Garnet! Come quickly! Bring the healer!" The voice roused Devin from a deep slumber. She leapt to her feet and ran out of Garnet's house, with Garnet at her shoulder, running too.

Anna was already running toward the commotion, along with several Heschtas. Other women were milling around, asking one another what had happened. Near the main hearth they saw Swain. She was covered in the blood of the man who she was helping. She lay him down gently, and looked up at Devin.

"It is Lexis. There are three more coming. They are injured too." Swain's voice held a bitterness that Devin had never heard.

Instantly, several women went running off toward the men's encampment to assist the others. Anna was already kneeling over Lexis, assessing his injuries. Devin knelt down beside the man, whose face was bruised and swollen almost beyond recognition.

"Lexis, my friend, what happened to you?" Devin asked him gently. She could not tell whether he was awake. She took his hand, offering support.

Slowly, the face turned toward her, and his lips moved. The voice was weak and rasping.

He said, "Falcone has gone mad. He plans to harm you. Beware."

Devin was stunned. She had been aware of the unrest in the men's encampment this season. But for it to have escalated to violence was unimaginable.

"Shhhh. You rest now." Anna scolded him. "You can speak later."

Garnet gently pulled Devin away from the injured man, and spoke softly. "Go and see what the other men can tell you. Leave Lexis to us, dear one."

Devin's shock was slowly subsiding. "Yes. I will go and see how I can assist the others."

Kelan had arrived, and followed as Devin trotted off in the direction the others had gone. Garnet turned back to assist Anna with their injured friend.

There were three more men approaching the village. Toban, Eli and Jonathon were met and assisted by the women. They had each been injured too, though Lexis was the worst. Kelan assessed the injuries and instructed that these be taken to the visitor's house and made comfortable. Once they were all inside and resting, she attended their various physical wounds. But the emotional wounds would take much longer to heal. While they were being cared for, Toban told Devin a shocking tale.

Apparently, Falcone had announced a plan to attack the women's village and steal food and furs for the winter. The idea had shocked the men. They could not fathom taking things from their sisters and mothers and friends. Certainly not in the violent manner that Falcone proposed. Lexis refused to entertain the idea, and said he thought that Falcone had gone mad. The other three had agreed, and stood up to Falcone alongside Lexis. Other men stood up next to their leader. Falcone had gone berserk then, and beaten Lexis with a log from the fire. A fight had ensued and the four had been driven from the encampment.

The women were stunned by the news. Certainly, Falcone had finally gone mad. Why would the men's tribe feel the need to steal anything? The women would have given them meat and cheese and furs for the winter, out of love and friendship. And why had only four of the tribe opposed Falcone's crazy ranting? Was he so violent that all the other men feared him?

"We will need to keep watch." Swain told Devin quietly. "If Falcone is coming, we will need to know it."

"Yes. Ask Nita and Tem to go with you. And tell them to bring their bows."

Swain nodded gravely and went to gather Tem and Nita.

Lexis was placed gently on a drag and carried to the healer's house. He would need constant care. Anna and Garnet would take turns staying with the man. Herta, Daña and Barde would assist them. Wren and Marjika brewed special broths with herbs and majik to strengthen him, and sat for hours holding his hand and talking to him of their children. The children were allowed to visit briefly several days later. And even though Lexis looked much better than he had the first several days, the girls cried at his injuries.

Over the next days, as Lexis began to heal, the Heschtas and the hunters kept watch. Toban, Eli and Jonathon insisted upon taking their turns at patrolling too. Devin instructed the women to allow it. She knew that the men felt helpless and victimized, and that doing something to assist the women would be beneficial to them. There was no sign of Falcone or anyone else.

Swain went to Devin on the fifth day, and said, "We need to know what Falcone is up to. Nita and I will sneak up on the men's village and see what we can learn. Tem and the three men will continue to watch from here."

"I will go with you." Devin insisted. "I cannot ask you and Nita to take such a risk alone. Though I agree we do need to know what is happening there."

"No, Devin." Swain disagreed. "The village needs you here. Nita and I know ways to be silent and invisible. We will come to no harm."

And so they set off as the sun disappeared that evening. Devin and Garnet advised Tem and the men of the trip. Jonathon had wanted to go along, but Garnet talked him out of it.

Devin had called for a village meeting to talk to everyone about what was happening. The three men who were able would continue to watch the perimeter of the village while the women talked.

Garnet stood near the main fire, watching the women gather. They were quiet and somber. She stood tall, smiling comfortingly at all who looked to greet her. She knew that during difficult times, she must be visible and confident. The tribe always looked to her for clues about their safety and comfort. She would present a calm and reassuring countenance, no matter how she felt inside.

When all had gathered, Devin spoke, "Everyone by now has heard what has happened. Everyone is sad and afraid. That is normal. But our village is safe. Our hunters and scout and the Heschtas have been keeping watch for any danger. And at this moment, two have gone to quietly approach the men's village. They will observe what is happening there and report to us in the morning."

"What of Lexis? Does he heal?" asked someone.

"He is healing. But his spirit still suffers." Anna answered. "I have advised him to take short walks starting tomorrow. When you see him, let him know that he is loved. This will help his healing."

~~~~

A few hours later and far from the village

center, Swain squatted behind the tree. She was motionless. Nita was a short distance away, lying flat in some tall grasses. It had taken them only a short time to come within long sight of the men's camp. It had taken them three times as long to approach it from there. Like all good scouts, they had moved only with the wind or other noise to cover their footfalls. They had guarded their shadows and kept out of sight. From this vantage point they could see most of the camp. Their plan was to stay in place until nightfall and then retreat.

The things they had seen around the men's camp told them much. There were drags piled with goods near the edge of the camp, as if someone would soon travel. And there was a spot further out where there was recently turned earth. A large rock marked the spot. The markings on the rock and the amulet that hung from it had told the women that old Dain had died. The men's custom was to bury the bodies of the dead in the earth. Sometimes the spot was marked. More often it was not.

The men's camp seemed lifeless as compared to the bustling village where the women lived. Only a few men moved around. Swain wondered where the rest of them had gone. Perhaps a hunt, she thought. But she had seen no large herds lately. It was no wonder, she mused, with all of the people patrolling around. The necessity to have watchers guarding the village would probably have scared off any herds that wandered nearby. If the men hunted, they would not be very near to the encampment or the village. And if they approached the village from any direction, the vigilant guard set up by the Heschtas would spot them.

Noise off to her left attracted her attention. She saw men filing out of a large tent. So, she thought, they had been holding a council. They scattered as they came out of the tent, each going his own way. Thankfully, none walked out of the camp toward the scouts. The men looked weary and sad to Swain's eyes. She wondered what had made them so dispirited. Nita was closer, and had excellent hearing. Perhaps she had heard something of their plans.

They waited until the commotion had subsided, and then crept away from the village.

Nita reported to Devin when they returned that the men planned to leave. They had decided that it was too risky to attack the women now that they were on guard. So they were planning to set out earlier than normal this year. They would go west and try to cross the mountains before winter, and then turn south. Nita said that the men did not plan to return to this area, ever.

The news was met with great sadness that evening by the women of the village and their visitors.

"Falcone will lead them to their deaths." Lexis lamented. "The men are misguided. Falcone has lost his wits. And what is everyone else thinking? They cannot believe that this plan is a good one."

"But for all the generations that we remember," Jonathan told him gently "We have followed a leader until his death. They are pledged to trust his judgment above their own. You know that. He cannot be removed, unless someone challenges him to fight to the death."

"Or until the healer invokes the law of advisement." Toban said quietly. The men all looked at the young healer, stunned. True, there was a law that said the village healer could rule if a leader was unfit. But it had happened only once before, and it was many generations ago. "But I do not know if that would work. I left the village so soon after Dain's death that no ceremony has been performed to name me healer."

"But everyone knows that it was Dain's wish for you to follow him." Lexis said.

"Let us leave this discussion for now." Jonathan suggested, turning to the women. "Perhaps the leaders of this village have some ideas."

Devin sighed, shaking her head sadly. "I am grieved. I do not know what we have done to infuriate them so."

"You have done nothing." Lexis reached out, touching the leader's forearm. "Falcone has lost his reason. And the men are confused."

"Perhaps we should simply remind them of their connection to us." Kelan offered.

Everyone looked at the girl. She went on, "If

it was any other year, and the men were readying to leave, what would we do?"

"But this is not every other year, dear." Herta added. "Not to Falcone."

"You see, that is the point exactly." Kelan became more animated as she spoke. "If we act like our feelings or actions have changed, then he seems to be correct in his ranting. If we act as we always have, treating the men with love and friendship, perhaps some of them will see that it is not us who has changed."

Her words were met with silence, save the crackling of the fire. She looked around the circle. Lexis was looking at her curiously. Toban was smiling and nodding. Garnet grinned.

"You are right, daughter." Garnet said. "If we act afraid or angry, it will only fuel his madness. We must be there when they leave, with gifts and smiles, as always."

"And what if he attacks you?" Jonathan asked, still reluctant to agree to this plan.

"If he tries to attack us" Devin leaned forward to make her point, "then he will look even more ridiculous than he does now. Our women can handle Falcone if we need to."

Several days later, when the scouts reported that the men were preparing to leave, the women and children walked out to meet them, carrying cheeses and gifts, as they always had. Lexis and the others hovered near the edges of the group at Devin's insistence. She thought that the sight of them may provoke Falcone.

A murmur of anticipation rippled through the crowd as the men came closer. Bard, standing amid the group began to sing, her clear voice carrying the tune.

"Fair ye well, my friends, on your long journey.
May the trails you walk be straight and true
May you be well while we are parted
ON your return, we'll welcome you."

The women joined in as she continued, and the song gained strength. As the men approached, some of the women waved to individuals whom they knew. Falcone, a fevered gleam in his eyes, marched past them as if they were not there. Some of the men, a tense set to their shoulders, eyes focused stiffly on the man ahead of them, followed him closely. Others walked more slowly, looking wistfully at their friends.

"Will you ignore the gifts of your friends?" Devin called loudly to them, her voice cutting through the song.

Falcone spun around and marched angrily toward her. "FRIENDS???? Since when are you my friend, woman??" His eyes held violent, aggressive look. His wiry hair, while thin on top, was bushy and stood out around the side of his head, giving him the look of a skinny crazed coyote.

Devin fought to keep her voice calm and look into his eyes. "We have always been friends and allies, Falcone. Nothing has changed, except you." She looked around at the men. Most of them looked down at their feet, as though they were ashamed of Falcone's behavior. Good, Devin thought. At least they see that his behavior is not normal.

Marjika stepped forward and tried to lay her hand on his bicep, saying "We are still your friends..."

At her touch, Falcone snapped. He flung her hand away as though it were the ember from a cooking fire, and lunged at her. From the crowd of men, a boy leapt forward, yelling "NO Falcone! You will not hurt my mother!" He jumped onto Falcone's back, crying and pounding on the man's shoulders. Falcone spun around, dislodging the boy, and began to beat him with his fists. Men surged forward, pulling Falcone off the boy, who now lay motionless. Marjika picked up the limp body, sobbing.

"WHY? Why would you harm a child???" she screamed at him.

Lexis and Toban stepped forward and stood between the woman and the men who were holding a still ranting Falcone. Lexis looked down at his son, tears running down his face and dripping off his strong chin. He raised his eyes slowly and stepped toward Falcone with a steely glint in his eyes. He felt a hand on his shoulder and turned his head. "No, Lexis. Do not become like him." Tem held his eyes for a moment before he laid his head on her shoulders and wept.

The men, unable to calm Falcone, dragged him away from the crowd and held him on the ground. Falcone still screamed "Traitors! Woman lovers! Are you not men???"

"Stop this madness!" Toban said in a tone that stopped all the noise around him. "What is happening here? How can we attack our mothers and daughters and friends, and kill one of our own sons? What are we becoming??" The tears glistened in his eyes, too. "Are we so entrenched in custom that we will follow this crazy man to our very destruction? How many more must die before you see the truth?"

Many of the men looked down, scuffing their feet in the dirt. Some others moved over to touch women they knew and to comfort and be comforted. Toban's calm voice carried over the crowd. "My brothers, Dain has passed on. I was his apprentice. Do you accept me as healer?"

The men, looking toward Toban indicated assent. "Then I invoke the law of advisement. As your healer, I deem Falcone unable to lead."

"NO!" a large burly man stepped through the crowd. "I do not recognize you or this travesty! You merely do as the women tell you!"

"Look at him." Toban said calmly, nodding

toward the struggling Falcone.

The leader continued to try to get away from the men who were holding him. "I am leader!" He screamed, spittle flying from his mouth. "You will follow me or you will follow another! Those traitors just want to lead the tribe!" He continued to try to pull away from his captors. He was covered in sweat and mud. He had urinated on himself. "I leave today, and I take nothing with me from this wicked place! These women seek to own you! You are not men if you do not follow! LET ME GO!!!" With a mighty thrust, he wrenched himself free. He stomped off across the meadow, still yelling. "If I am your leader, follow me! If you are led by women, then stay and suckle!!!!"

Most of the men looked uneasy, shuffling their feet and looking around. Some followed Falcone, dragging what supplies they could along with them. The assemblage watched them march away.

"I think two scouts should follow them to make sure they keep going and do not return to attack us." Lexis suggested.

"I will go." Jonathan offered.

"I will go too." added Swain.

Looking to the remaining men, Devin spoke. "I am sorry for your loss" she said quietly, taking the boy gently from Marjika and placing him in Jonathan's arms. "We offer any help you may need."

"Thank you, Devin." Toban answered for the

men. "But we must give the boy an honorable ceremony. And we must choose a new leader." Turning to the remaining men, he said "I think we should all go home now."

The men who had been standing with their loved ones in the women's tribe reluctantly turned to follow the others back to their camp.

"We should go home too." Devin told the women. Several of them helped Marjika stand, and guided her gently toward the village.

After following the group to the edge of the flat lands, the two scouts had decided it was time to return home. Falcone's men had set up a camp and it looked to both scouts like they would stay put for a while. They had followed Falcone's men for two days and nights. Now, on the third night, they were part of the way home, and bone tired.

The small fire crackled as the fat from the rabbit they had caught dripped on the scarlet embers and produced a fragrant wisp of smoke. Jonathan turned the roast over again, so it would cook evenly. He gave a tentative prod to the tubers that lie wrapped in leaves amid the hot coals. They would be soft soon. The slow rhythmic shushing sound of Swain's knife was comforting as she sharpened the blade with the stone.

He looked up, the smoke making him squint. He watched her practiced movements, the smooth track that her hand followed on each pass as she held the blade at a precise angle. They had spoken only rarely on this trip, each dealing with grief in their own way. He wondered if she was ready to talk. Her eyes flicked from the blade to Jonathan's. The hands stopped.

"Dinner is almost ready." He said gently.

"Good." She smiled a little, putting her tools away and rubbing her hands together. "We covered a lot of ground today. I am hungry. Thank you for cooking."

"It was my turn." He said simply. "Thank YOU for catching it." He paused, deciding if he should talk more. "We should see the villages sometime tomorrow."

"Yes. We can make our report and relax for a few days. I will stay with the Heschtas for a while. I need to renew my equipment, and my heart. Astaga will help me. What will you do?"

He was encouraged by her reply. She had spoken more words than they had exchanged in the whole trip. He handed her a portion of the rabbit and answered, "I do not know. I will return to our camp and see what needs to be done. I will serve in whatever way is needed."

She nodded, understanding. Neither scout's temperament allowed them to share their weariness of heart out loud, but in their silence, they had shared the grief. She looked at him for a long moment. "Jonathan. I would travel again with you. You are a fine scout."

He dipped his chin in acknowledgment of the moment. "I would travel with you again too, my friend. Perhaps we should speak with our tribes about scouting and hunting together sometimes when we are camping nearby."

"So you assume that your people will travel this winter?" she asked.

"Of course. We are not meant to stay in one place." He chewed thoughtfully on his meat. "Staying in one place makes your tribe happy. And it provides a sheltered place to raise babies. But our tribe's young ones are of choosing age, not small ones. I do not think any of the men would feel happy staying in one place."

"What about the old ones?" she asked him. "The last time I saw Dain, Toban was carrying him like an infant. We would have gladly sheltered him."

Jonathan nodded. "We know, Swain. But the old man's dignity would not have been preserved by staying in the village. No man wants to admit that he cannot care for himself or his people. It is in our blood. Dain knew what he was choosing. We respected it."

"Tell me the story of the Toads." she asked him, settling back to enjoy a tale. She stretched her tired feet toward the crackle of the fire, warming them.

He sighed, shaking his head ruefully, but his eyes twinkled with the flicker of the fire. "You know the story."

"But you tell it well." she chided.

He looked down at the ground, and his face became serious. "The men may discover a new messenger. I think many will associate the Toad with Falcone now. Before I left, Lexis pleaded with me at council to take him along. He said that he wanted to go "Toad hunting". I promised Toban that I would watch out and intercept him if we saw him following Falcone."

Her laughter startled him. Her wrist snapped outward suddenly as she threw the leg bone she had been chewing on into the fire.

"Before I left the women's camp, the Heschtas called me to their fire circle and asked me to watch out for the same thing. They were planning to try to get him involved in a project for the youngsters to hold his attention. I wish we could have brought him along. Perhaps being out in the woods would help. It helps me." she looked at him directly. She had shared a feeling with him.

His crooked smile and nod gave her answer. " Sometimes I just have to get out on my own. A scout's trait, I suppose."

"You are right, brother. We should take hunts and hikes together once in a while. Perhaps you and I can go on a walk and fish for Salmon in the waterfalls. We could ask Wren to smoke them for your winter trip."

"I would bet that some of the men would be willing to gather firewood in exchange for the food." he predicted.

"Good." she bobbed her chin, signaling a deal. "We can bring it up to our councils when we make our report."

He wiped his hands on the grass and stood. "I will lay out our bedrolls."

She nodded and leaned forward to cover the little fire with ash and dirt. Small puffs of ash rose up as she patted the mound with the flat of her big knife. Once the embers were extinguished she rose and walked the short distance to the place from which the sounds of rustling hides had come. No member of either tribe would sleep so near a cooking fire lest predators, attracted by the warm smell of food, would enter the camp. Most animals would avoid humans even if they were sleeping, but a large animal enticed by the smell of meat could be dangerous.

Jonathan looked up as she quietly approached, then lay down on his bedroll and turned to face away from her. She settled into her own sleeping nest and turned her back to him, letting the quiet sounds of the night lull her to sleep.

~~~~

"Time to awaken, little one." Ashe whispered to the sleeping girl.

Ara sat up, scrubbing her scalp with her fingers. "It's time to start cooking?"

"It is."

She followed the lean brown form toward the cooking fires through the thinning darkness. She could make out other quiet forms moving in the same direction.

The festival campsite had grown exponentially in the days since their arrival. Many more travel parties of workers had arrived, increasing the pace of the preparations. The area now looked like Ara's village had in the first few weeks that her people had lived there. It was an organized cluster of hide tents, huddled around several large cleared areas that were fast becoming the dance ground, the teaching grounds, the hearth and the commons. Ashe and Ara wound their way silently past the dark tents toward the cooking area that the women commonly called the hearth.

It was a hive of activity. There were several workers bustling about, tending three separate cooking circles. Ara had helped set the rings of stones for the fires. The largest was egg shaped seven paces across at the fat end, four paces across at the thin end, and thirteen paces long. It was surrounded by two rings of head-sized stones. The inner ring marked the edge of the fire. The stones were already blackened in places. The outer ring of stones marked off a walkway around the fire. This was the cooks' domain. The stones of the outer wall were still their natural colors, mostly gray or brown. Four large stones with flattened tops lay atop stone pillars at each direction. These were used as work tables for the cooks. Next to each large stone was a water skin that was used both for cooking, and to wash the top of the stone periodically. The large stones, which were as high as Ara's ribs, had already been there when they arrived. Uba-kala told the girls that the stones remained in place always. When the women were not there, the stones stood as silent sentinels, protecting the land. Ara thought it was wonderful that the women left offerings on the tops of the stones when the gathering was done, to thank the local spirits for hosting their visit again.

Ashe plopped down next to the scout on one of the many logs that loosely surrounded the hearth, and was handed a cup of warm broth. The nighttime scouts would be going to their sleeping nest soon. Awakening the cooks was their final duty for the night. Ara had not been to the scout's nest like Jori, but she knew it was a short distance away from the main gathering, and that the scouts slept and kept watch in two shifts.

She hurried to the main fire and sought out Mare, the woman who organized the morning meals. Ara found the pale round woman standing near some youngsters who were cutting up tubers. She did not speak the same language as Mare, but understood the gestures she made. Ara liked the spark of fire that glinted merrily in the woman's eyes. That same spark seemed to be reflected in her wild red hair. This morning, Mare made a stirring motion and pointed to a cauldron on the thin end of the big fire circle, opposite the fat end where the big roasting spit already turned.

Ara nodded, smiling and turned to stir the "porridge". The thick soupy substance was new to Ara. It was made with something called "oats" that

Mare had brought all the way from her homeland far to the north. To the oats, Mare added honey from her own northern tribe, and nuts that had been brought by a tribe from the lush green lands near the warm sea to the south.

Ara liked the taste of the sticky stew. She couldn't eat very much of it before her belly was full. Ara supposed that in the cold northern land where Mare's people lived, having a warm filling breakfast was important. Ara, like most of her own tribe, ate a small portion of fruit in the morning, sometimes with a bite of cheese or flat bread. But she thought that having some of the porridge on a cold winter's morning sounded good. Perhaps they could trade something for some seeds of the oat plant, and try growing it near their village. She would talk it over with Jori later.

Tan, one of the other cooks, approached carrying a bundle. She smiled, "good morning Ara. I've some nuts for the porridge." She poured a measure of the chopped nuts into the cauldron as Ara continued to slowly stir. "Good morning, Tan." Ara smiled up at the lanky woman. "Did you chop nuts all night long?"

"It seems so." Tan replied, finishing her task and turning away. "And now I must go on to my next assignment."

A whistled signal made them all turn and look to the east. The glow of the rising sun shimmered on the horizon, illuminating several shapes that moved toward the encampment. Ara recognized Jori's ambling gait. She was walking beside a very tall figure that could only have been the scout, Swain. As the little group approached, Ara waived, her heart rejoicing at the sight of her tribe mates. But there were only four. Ara knew that many more had planned to attend the gathering this season. What could have delayed the rest of the women? She swung the big pot to the side of the fire to keep warm, and went to meet them.

"Hello!" she shouted, running up to the little group.

"Hello, Ara!" Said Marjika, pulling the girl into a warm hug. "You have grown taller!"

The girl looked into the faces of the others as she was released. She sensed their tension. "What has happened?"

Jori's arm coiled protectively around her shoulders, "there has been trouble at home." She explained.

A jolt of alarm coursed through Ara. "Is someone ill? What has happened?"

"Everyone is safe now." Petrov reassured her. "We will tell you about it once we have rested. But we are the only ones who will come to the gathering this season, and only for a short time."

Remembering how far the little party must have traveled, Ara momentarily suppressed her curiosity. "Come and have some breakfast. Then I will help you set up your tents."

"We cannot stay that long, little one." Marjika told the girl. "We will sleep in the scout's nest for a night or two, but then we must return to the village. We only came to warn the other Tribes of a danger."

Though she was truly alarmed now, Ara led them to the hearth and served them bowls of the porridge she had helped to make.

As the women ate, they told her the story of Falcone's actions. The girl was stunned and saddened by the incident, and relieved that more of her people had not been harmed. At Jori's request, Ara went looking for Norahjen, Uba-kala, and the other women from her own village, so they could meet with the party at the scout's nest and hear the tale.

"You were right to come and warn us" Norahjen told the scouts. "Falcone could have changed direction and come this way. Our scouting teams should be alerted. And the other Tribes must be aware of his insanity, so that they can keep watch in case he attacks one of them. I will call a meeting of the Queens this afternoon and let everyone know."

"I still cannot take it all in." Ara said sadly. "Falcone was always a good friend to our Tribe, and a good father. How could he have changed so drastically?"

"I do not know what changed him, but he is not the man you knew. Swain said gently. "The Falcone who held you in his lap when you were a little girl is gone, and in his place a madman has emerged. Even his facial expressions are different."

"I grieve the losses, too." Jori added. "But his madness is something none of us can understand.

He was never a very logical man. His emotions always drove him. Now we must simply protect our people, and move on from here. What is happening with the men now?"

"Lexis leads the men now." Marjika told them all. "He is a rational and kind man who will be a good leader. And Toban is the new healer, who advises their leader in most things. They have chosen to release their connection with the Toad Spirit and seek out a new spirit guide for their Tribe. Toban has gone to the mountains to meditate and bring back a new totem for them all. They also intend to rotate the leadership every few years, so that no one is leader until death."

"Did the Toad spirit tell Falcone to attack the women?" Ara was horrified at the thought of any totem spirit becoming violent."

"No, child." Swain explained. "None of the men said that. It is just that they want to start fresh, with a new way and a new symbol."

"Perhaps you should return home with the scouts." Uba-kala suggested. "It would comfort your mothers to have you with them."

"But we said we would help you set up the encampment." Jori protested.

"And so you did, my young friend." Uba-kala made a wide sweep with her arm. "Look around you. The camp is ready. I am grateful for your help. But you are needed at home."

"So it is settled. We will stay tonight and tomorrow, and then leave for home when the sun comes up again." Swain told them.

"I will come too." Norahjen looked at Uba-kala, who nodded. "I wish to assure myself that all is well with my people."

Fall 1986 C.E.

Brown and red leaves crunched under my feet, swirling and falling into the old stone stairway when I lifted the heavy door. It made a heavy thump as I swung it open to lie flat on the hard ground. I muscled the armload of pumpkins down the cracked old stone steps into the root cellar and lined them up behind the others I had placed there the day before. The open doorway allowed a dim yellow ray of light to touch the fronts of the shelf lined wall, and cast shadows across the recessed corners. The light suddenly vanished and I turned toward the stairway to see what blocked my light source.

"Make sure you are leaving enough room between the pumpkins." The old woman's croaking voice reminded me. "We will bring the kartof next."

She backed up a few steps as I ascended into the cool morning. "Kartof?" I asked.

"Kartof, kartof!" annoyed at my stupidity, she pointed.

"Kartof." She said. "Put them in the nets above the shelving. Take the lantern down there so you can see."

She hobbled back toward the outdoor hearth, where she had been busy this morning, making something that smelled like molasses and cinnamon. I returned to my task.

We had been harvesting her large garden for weeks now, first picking and preserving the tomatoes and peppers, then gathering the beans, onions and peas, and now the squash pumpkin and potatoes. Anna had said we would take in the apples last. Probably tomorrow. I wasn't looking forward to climbing those gnarled old trees, but I was sure the fruit would be welcome when the cold time came.

That evening, as she served me a portion of her wonderful stew, she said "At this time of year, the veil between the worlds is thin. It is the time for omens and warnings. I tell you this: if you receive a warning, do not overlook it. The consequence can be severe."

I looked up at her, studying the sadness that had overcome her features. "You have experienced these consequences?" I asked.

"Yes. And it cost us many lives over many generations." She said sadly. "Looking back, we realized that the first incident was a warning. One we took seriously for a time. But as time passed, the danger did not seem imminent, and we let our guard down and became comfortable, thinking that we were safe. We were not." Her dark eyes glistened with remembered loss. "As you walk through the world, young leader, do not be deceived by those who would come in the guise of friendship only to betray you. Trust your own people wholly, but beware of those who say they are allies until they have proven their loyalty with their deeds."

Try as I might, I could not persuade her to say more.

Fall, 3778 B.C.E.

The morning breeze had turned cold. The sun was warm, but the wind was cool enough to raise little bumps on Jori's forearm as it moved in the smooth rhythmic motions of blade sharpening.

"So how do they get the honey out of the hives without being attacked?" she asked the big scout.

"They use smoke." Norahjen explained. "Apparently, smoke calms the bees, and then they don't react to the jostling. Nami said that after a time, the bees also got used to her, and now they never become alarmed when she approaches."

"It's an interesting idea." Jori admitted, "And mother did teach us last spring that a garden full of bees was an indicator of a good crop."

"Also, we can use honey as a trade item."

The scout added. "I think it is worth looking into."

"What is worth looking into?" the silky voice asked. Garnet had silently approached them from behind. "Did I startle you?"

"Of course not." Norahjen blustered. "I felt your presence."

Garnet smiled.

"We were talking about bee keeping." Jori told her. "One of the women from across the sea told Norahjen that they build places for the bees to live near their village so they don't have to go hunting for honey."

"Have you mentioned this to Devin?" the Queen asked. She was reminded again of the similarities between Devin and Jori. When Devin was young, she had found a pair of orphaned puppies and taken them in. Over the years, she had trained them to do any number of simple tasks. They lived with her still. During her childhood Jori, too, had brought home lost or injured animals to be cared for and healed. And she had played for many hours in the storage area with the cats.

"Not yet. I wanted to hear more of the story first." Jori told her.

"The world is changing." Norahjen looked out across the flats that bordered the village. "All the tribes used to travel to find things. Now we all seem to want to stay in one place and bring the things to us instead. We plant gardens, train dogs, and now perhaps keep bees. I do not know if it is wise."

"Do you regret settling here?" Garnet was

surprised by the remark.

"No. We are well fed and have fewer injuries than when we were traveling. But we are changing the structure of nature... Moving things around to suit our needs, perhaps at the expense of other beings. I often wonder if we shouldn't just leave things where the Mother put them." Norahjen chuckled. "I am beginning to sound like old Shayana. Perhaps I need a good walk." She unfolded her long legs and stood stretching. "I will go to the hills and look for a herd for the hunters."

Watching the big scout go, Jori asked, "What do you think mother? Should we try to build a bee garden?"

"I think you should investigate the idea. Talk with Devin and more with Norahjen. The bees will be going into their winter hibernation soon. Perhaps we can relocate a hive in the late winter to a place close to our gardens. It may be that moving them while they are in their winter sleep time would minimize any disruption to their tribe."

"I will talk with Devin about it." Jori told her.

"Do you have many chores today?"

"Just these blades to sharpen, why?"

"Some of the children would like to go out for a walk this afternoon and gather materials for their masks for the harvest day feast. Would you like to come and assist me?" Garnet asked.

Jori looked up at her mother, furrowing her brow. She knew that Garnet needed no help in as simple a walk as this. There must be some other reason for her to ask Jori to come along. Still, if Garnet had wanted to explain, she would have. Jori shrugged and said simply, "Of course. I could use a short walk."

"Good. Would you come to the main hearth when you are finished? I will meet you there." She rose and walked away.

Jori put the finishing touches on the blade she was sharpening and put away her tools. She arrived at the hearth as Garnet was instructing a small group of children.

"You will stay close enough to me at all times that I can see you. And you will go everywhere in pairs. Can you tell me why, Micah?"

"In case someone is hurt, the other one can help." The boy blurted out excitedly.

"Good! Jori will be coming with us today too." The children looked up smiling at the tall warrior.

She smiled back, "OK, let us be off!"

The little party crossed the river using the new log structure that Devin had put in place this summer. The "bridge" consisted simply of three tree trunks, with branches removed, lashed together with ropes made of tall grass, laying side by side across from one bank of the little river to the other.

It certainly kept the children's feet dryer, Garnet mused, as she walked gingerly across the bumpy surface, but balancing yourself while walking across it was definitely an acquired skill. Many of the women had ended up in the water when they first tried to cross.

As they walked across the flats, the children began to spread out, each looking for something that they could fashion into a mask or disguise for the upcoming feast day. The sun shone warm on the little party, and there was a soft breeze. Garnet looked to the East, where the gentle foothills of the mountain range made a silvery backdrop to the scene. She led them downstream in a wide arc, strolling slowly through the knee- high grasses. Jori, watching her mother, sensed unease. Finally she spoke.

"What is it? You are troubled."

"I do not know, Jori. I have a sense of something coming. Something not…right. I do not understand what I am seeing." Garnet admitted. "I have been dreaming of smoke. Not mist, or fog, but acrid smoke."

"Have you sought out advice from anyone?"

"I am." Garnet smiled at her. "What do you think?"

Jori was stunned. Garnet was asking for her opinion. After staring open mouthed a moment at her mother, she said, "I think we should have a look at every fire in the village and make sure they are all secure. That is the thing I would do to protect the physical village."

Garnet nodded.

"AND we should tell the Heschtas immediately. The danger may not be physical. Also, there may be more women having these kinds of dreams." Jori looked at her pointedly.

Garnet sighed. "I suppose you are correct. We can go and see them as soon as we return."

"Look!" Little Matra came running up to them, holding some large feathers. "I can be an owl!"

Jori took the feathers the child held up to her and examined them. "Yes. These are from an owl. That is a very lucky find! Owls do not gift us with their feathers very often."

The dark haired child grinned happily at the women, swaying from foot to foot in her excitement. "Perhaps I will gift them to Marjika when I am done using them."

"Good girl!" Garnet smiled "That is a fine idea.
"

"Herta may be able to use these to feather hunting arrows, Matra, if Marjika has no need of them." Jori told the girl.

Micah and Zusza also found treasures in the grass, and they returned happily to the village a short time later to begin creating their costumes for the feast day.

Garnet and Jori walked over to the Heschtas' fire to tell them of Garnet's dream and to seek out advice of the group.

The Heschtas thought it wise to send a team to every fire in the village to check for safety. They also decided to perform a protective spell around the perimeter, and to send out extra scouts for the time being. When Garnet had told the women of her feelings, they had immediately begun to make plans. They trusted the intuition of the Queen.

The group decided to send Bard around the village with a message for everyone to be particularly careful of fire. They did not wish to alarm the Tribe, so they made a message that simply spoke of the danger of fire in the dry weather of autumn. The made sure that there was a skin of water hanging near the entrance to each building. They also planned to perform magic on the night of the harvest day feast.

The harvest celebration was always held on the day of the fall Equinox, when the length of day and night were equal. It was a good night to do protective magic, and the Heschtas decided that they would hold a small ritual at the Temple for just that purpose.

Satisfied with the precautions that were underway, Garnet walked toward the smoking house to see how the preparations for the cold months were coming. Wren was just coming out as Garnet approached and greeted the Queen cheerfully.

"Ah, Garnet. How are you on this fine day?" she asked, smiling.

"I am well, my friend." Garnet answered, touching the cook amicably, "How are things here?"

"We have meats and cheeses hanging that almost fill the space. The hunters have been very productive this season, and the men have provided much milk from the hills." Wren said proudly." We will have plenty for ourselves and for trade. I was just going to go over to the grinding area to see how my new apprentices are doing there. Would you care to come along and see?"

Garnet fell into step with her friend. "I have had premonition about fire." She told wren "And the Heschtas will be asking everyone to be extra vigilant around our fire circles."

The big cook nodded. "I will counsel all my women to be careful. And we will build up the sand piles too." Wren's crews kept sand piles within a few steps of each large hearth, to smother any fire that got out of its circle.

Not wishing to offend her friend, Garnet said "I know that your training stresses fire safety, and that you insist upon a wide clear area around any cooking fire. The danger probably does not come from within the village."

Wren smiled, throwing her arm around the Queen's shoulder. "It does not hurt to remind everyone to be careful, Garnet. Even the most carefully constructed stew can be ruined by inattention."

The pair ducked into the grinding hut, causing the women there to look up and smile. It was a bustling scene, with several women working together. Some women turned the big wheel; some swept the ground grain into baskets to be carried to the filling station. Others poured the ground grain into large bags of woven grasses. The bags, once filled, were sewn shut and placed on a drag to be taken to the storage area. Garnet made a few encouraging remarks to the workers, turning with Wren toward the main storage huts.

"I don't think you have seen these large nets yet, have you?" Wren asked as they ducked through the low door into the dark little root storage room. She pointed, indicating long nets that were stretched across the space. The nets were narrow at each end, and fastened high up on the walls. The middle of the nets was wider, and rolled around, almost like a tube. Kartof roots were lined up neatly in rows in the first several nets, and beets were lined in others. A black cat perched neatly on top of one net.

"Ara learned from Mare at the Gather about these nets. In Mare's homeland, called Eire, Kartof are called "potatoes" and they call these nets "hammocks". They use these nets to store their kartof and other root vegetables in the cold months. They say that allowing the roots to be touched by the cold air instead of lying in a pile helps them last longer. And when they travel, they simply take the two ends of the net, tie them together and they have a carrying net. Mare even took the time to show Ara how they were made."

"So we are trying Mare's method this season? How wonderful!" Garnet smiled, pleased at the innovation. "And they give our feline helpers a perch from which to hunt! How were these nets made?"

"We had the children gather the grasses from near the river. We used the ones with the fibrous bulbs on the top, because their stems are sturdy and pliable. And we save the bulbs for kindling. Then we weaved them into cords, and then used the cordage to weave into these loose nets. See how big the holes are? You can make them larger or smaller, depending upon what you want them to keep. And Ashe told the girl that in HER country, nets like this with weights on the ends are used for fishing! Devin is working on that theory."

"Oh. THAT'S what she was dragging toward the bank this morning!" Garnet laughed. "Perhaps I will go and have a look."

Garnet strolled toward the river and followed the path that she had seen Devin take as the sun rose. Not too far downstream, she spotted Devin and Tem. Devin was hip deep in the water, pulling one end of her net toward the shore. Tem held the other end, fastening it to a tree on the opposite bank. Garnet went to the edge and reached out, taking the end of rope and helping to pull.

"Ah. Thank you, love. Come to see my experiment?" Devin kissed her briefly and began to tie the end of the rope to a large fallen log.

"I did. Can you explain how it should work?" Garnet sat down on the log.

Tem waded across the water and joined them.

"I attached heavy stones along the bottom edge of the square to hold it down in the water, and suspended the top end along the surface of the water. I will leave this net in place today, and in the morning, I will roll it back in. Ashe said the fish can't swim through the netting, and get caught." Devin explained.

"We learn much from our sister tribes, do we not?" Garnet smiled.

"We do." Tem agreed. "Ashe even gave us some of those little shiny things to tie onto the top edge. She called them 'bells'. When you shake them, they make a sound. She said it would alert us if the net caught something very large, or was jerked hard. See?" She reached out and gave the end of the net a few hard pulls. There was a tinkling sound with the movement.

Garnet shook her head, smiling…"So, not only will you have the fish catch themselves, but you will have them tell you when they do so."

"Yes." Devin beamed. "That is, if it works here the same way it does in Ashe's camp. We will know in the morning."

Before dawn the next morning, Devin was awakened by the sound of the bells. They were ringing violently, as though something very large had been fouled in the net. She rose, grabbing her club and bow in case it was a bear, and ran toward the sound. She sensed several others following her to the river. She yelled "Sounds like a bear got caught in the nets! Let us see if we can help it!"

As they approached, they saw not fish or bears in the net, but men! Three men flailed in the water, their legs tangled in the nets. Devin dropped her bow and jumped in, trying to assist the closest one. As she reached for him, he raised a club and swung it at her. She ducked and so it missed her head, but landed painfully on her shoulder.

"Back up!" Devin heard Swain yell. She pushed with her legs away from the man, and felt a strong arm grasp her shoulders, pulling her out of the water. She regained her feet and looked around to see Jori, Garnet and Wren on the bank. Jori had her bow and was aiming at one of the men; Devin picked up her own bow and did the same. Wren picked up Devin's club.

Loudly, Garnet said "Stop struggling! Put down your weapons and be still or we will shoot at you!"

The men stood still, but the biggest one glared at them angrily.

"What are you doing there?" Devin asked them.

The big one spat into the water. "You'll see soon enough, stupid woman! We will burn your village to the ground, and take what is left as reward!"

Just then, the village seemed to erupt in noise: Women shouting or screaming, Bard blowing the alarm, men yelling, dogs barking and children crying. Garnet and Devin left Jori and Wren to deal with the men in the nets, and ran toward the center hearth, followed by the scout.

Marjika ran past them, herding the several

young ones toward the children's hut. The eyes of the girls were wide and they were crying. They barely noticed the group rushing past them toward the fray.

The Heschtas were on the opposite edge of the village circle, between the storage huts and the smoking hut. They were in a line, side by side and were resisting a line of men who were trying to get past them and into the center of the village. Falcone lay on his back, unconscious. He had blood streaming from his nose. The other men were advancing, swinging weapons or tools.

Devin quickly sent Tem with one group of women around the storage huts to the left of the Heschtas, and led the remaining women around the smoke hut to their right. Garnet would hold the center ground with Swain and the main group. Devin's idea was to come round the men from the sides, like they would with a herd of elk they were hunting. She hoped that if they surrounded the men, leaving only the rear for an escape that the men would flee.

The men were swinging long clubs and thrusting with long spears at the women, injuring several and shouting loudly. One woman cried out as a spear was thrust through her shoulder, blood spurting out and splashing down the front of her tunic. She fell back, and another warrior took her place, swinging a club at the man who had thrown the spear and knocking him to the ground. The women fought back with whatever was in their hands. Some had weapons or clubs, others had sticks or rocks. The men advanced again, and two entered the smoking hut. Women poured in after them.

Inside, Riala picked up a burning log and was swinging it to keep the men well back from the hearth. One man dropped to the ground and rolled at the cook, knocking her down. He picked up the burning log and smashed it down on the Riala's unprotected face. Then he ran outside, and thrust the burning log part way through the wall of the grinding hut! The wall erupted into flame, and the man ran toward the center of the village.

The combined efforts of the women had scattered the attackers, who now ran through the village in pairs or alone, damaging anything they could find and trying to injure any women they saw. One grabbed a small woman by the wrist and was dragging her away. He released her wrist only when Herta shot an arrow and hit him in the arm. Two of them picked up Falcone and dragged him out of the village. As they retreated, they ducked into houses and huts, stealing what they could find and carrying it off. Small groups of women pursued them, stopping only when the men cleared the edge of the village and kept going.

Devin's dogs attacked one man who was trying to enter the children's hut. They snarled and barked and even bit at his legs and arms. He swung his club at them, hitting one and knocking her unconscious. But before he could swing again,

Marjika materialized in the doorway of the hut and fired an arrow, hitting him in the throat. He clutched at the arrow; making gurgling sounds, and fell to the ground, dead. She stood there, frozen in place; shocked at having taken any life, let alone a human one.

Astaga, Herta and Kelan were patrolling the village circle, looking for any other attackers. They heard the dogs and came to assist. Herta dragged the body away toward the edge of the village. Kelan, her eyes moist with compassion, hugged Marjika, gently taking the bow from her hand and handed it to Astaga. The toolmaker added an arrow and reached past the women, leaning it against the wall of the hut just inside the door.

"You two go on patrolling" she told them. "I will stay here with Marjika and the children." Kelan spoke softly to the woman, guiding her inside.

Barde's big voice cut through the noise, saying "all come to the hearth!"

Astaga instructed Kelan and Marjika to stay where they were, and went with Herta to the big central hearth fire to see what the announcement was about.

On one side of the big central fires, several women sat or lie down, being tended by Anna and her apprentices. On the other, Devin stood with Garnet, organizing the women.

"We will need three teams of three to patrol the area and make sure all of the attackers are well away. Herta, Dana and Tem, pick your teams and go. Report back as soon as you know anything."

The three women each tapped two and briefly consulted before heading out in different directions.

"Ara, would you please go and see what Wren has done with the men in the river?? Report back right away."

Ara nodded and ran toward the place where Devin had cast her net the night before.

"Fires have been put out in both storage sheds and the smoking hut. I need you builders to go and assess the damage and see what repairs we can make."

Several women went off in that direction.

"Where is Kelan?" Garnet asked.

"She is with Marjika in the children's hut. One of them tried to attack there, but the dogs warned her and Marjika shot him with an arrow and saved the children. Marjika is in shock, I think. Kelan stayed to comfort her and the children."

Garnet signaled to another woman and they went off toward the children's hut.

Devin turned toward the other side of the fire. "Anna?"

Anna yelled over her shoulder "six injured; one badly. We will need drags to carry them to the central house where we can care for them all at once."

Ara ran back in, followed by Wren. "The men got free of the net and ran away. They were allowed to flee, as they were not attacking. But the dogs chased them. " She told Devin.

"Good. Will you go and assist the builders?"

By nightfall, the village had been secured. Both storage huts had been badly damaged and much food had been lost. The smoking hut was intact, but the stone walls were blackened and parts of the roof were gone. The grinding hut was badly damaged. The one wall that was still wood was nearly gone. The grinding wheel was not damaged, but the nut flour, sitting in baskets near the wall, had burned quickly. No cats had been found. Apparently they had fled the loud noises. The six injured women were cared for and would recover, though Riala, the brave cook's apprentice would carry burn scars on her face. Thankfully, the fire had missed her eyes. Norahjen had been shot just above the knee with an arrow. There were broken bones, but Anna thought that the wound would heal in time.

It was established that the attackers were Falcone's men. Several had been recognized. Nita was the only person present who had actually seen Falcone.

"He was ranting on about how his men were going to teach us our "place" in the world. He said no woman could ever stop him. That's when Tem hit him." The crafter smiled at the memory. "She swung her fist at him with every ounce of her weight behind it. Hit him so hard he flew up to here" she indicated knee height "and fell to the ground, completely unconscious with blood pouring from his nose." She was chuckling now. "Tem said 'any woman can stop you, little toad'. And then she just stepped over him and went after the next one, calm as can be." Devin heard the story with a grin, but did not comment.

Jori had run to the men's camp to warn them, and Toban and Lexis had returned with her to see how the men could assist. The attackers had not gone to the men's camp. Devin asked for few of the men to help with patrolling the area in case they came back. The men agreed, saying that they should coordinate patrols for their mutual protection. As they discussed the rotation, Kelan arrived with Marjika and the children. When Toban saw Kelan safe, he hugged her in front of everyone. Micah giggled.

The children were settled near the fire, and given a small task to do with the aid of one of the elders. Kelan touched Garnet's shoulder and whispered in her ear; they both went outside.

The two women walked slowly around the village circle, talking.

"Marjika still has not spoken." Kelan told her mother. "Anna says she is shocked at having killed a person. She responds to directions, sat down near the fire when I asked her to, but she will not speak. She did not even smile when Micah climbed into her lap."

"I think all we can do for her right now is to keep her warm and safe. I will ask Lexis to sit with her for a while. Perhaps she will speak to him."

Garnet said. "Are the children affected?"

"They do not seem to be. I do not think they saw anything much. Marjika was in the doorway, and she had them huddled under a fur near the wall. She saved their lives, you know."

"That is likely. We should plan a ritual to rid all the women of the fear and uncertainty they are experiencing. And we should do it soon." Garnet told the girl.

"We can talk more about that tomorrow. Tonight we all need to rest." Kelan said.

Devin's dogs came wagging up to the women, sniffing at their ankles and looking for affection. Kelan stopped to look at the one that had been struck by the man. "Devin says the dog is fine. She was knocked unconscious, but when she awakened, she seemed normal. They are good warriors!"

"Yes. They are so resilient!" Garnet laughed as one of the dogs jumped up on her, trying to lick her face.

"The children said that's how Marjika knew there was someone there. The dogs' barking alerted her, and she loaded her bow and went to the door. They seemed to know that he intended to hurt the children."

Giving the dog one last pat and turning away, Garnet admitted "yes, they have proven themselves loyal and useful, even if they are annoying at times. "

They strolled on, chatting about what their

next actions should be. As they came around to the side of the village where the burned huts were visible, they stopped, staring at the devastation that had been done. Garnet's eyes filled with tears. So much damage!

Wren came out of one of the storage huts and approached them. "We have lost about half of the herbs and dried produce. All of the flour we had ground is gone. About a quarter of the kartof were roasted by the fire. We can eat some of them while they last. Others were burned too badly to eat. Most of the smoked cheeses and meats are still good. They took the hanging boar shanks, a leg of elk and some cheeses. They did not take any fish that I can see. I suppose that is easy for them to catch. Some of the smoked fish was blackened and will have to be replaced. But we will not be getting any more goats' milk in trade until spring, so the few cheeses we have left are all there will be."

"We had not finished harvesting the onions and cabbage. We need to get that in and see where we stand for the winter." Garnet said thoughtfully. "And we may be able to find more of the nuts to grind. I am sure Jori will want to hunt to replace the meats."

"We must replace what we can and mete it out carefully if we are to be healthy this winter. Tomorrow, we will all sit down and make a plan." Kelan said. "But the sun is down now, and everyone must rest. Let us take some smoked fish and cheese and roasted kartof to the big hut, and then settle in for sleep."

The women, with help from Wren's apprentice Riala, loaded up a drag with the food and carried it to the central hut. Riala saw to it that everyone had some food. Garnet and Kelan saw to it that everyone stopped working and tried to get some sleep.

Except for the Heschtas. The Guardians of the village did not sleep; they watched.

One lone outdoor fire shone through the night, a beacon and a communication hub for the watchers who patrolled the area. The three teams were instructed to check in at the heschta's fire. Attending that position, Petrov sat, feeding sticks into the blaze, and drumming softly. She beat a heartbeat in the dark to soothe frazzled nerves. She stared pensively into the dancing flames as she patted her drum.

The world had changed today, she realized. Gone were the days (at least for now) when one or two lone scouts in a nest could keep an eye on the village. Tomorrow, they would have to set up a system of defense. And the idea of needing defense against other people was a very elemental change that would take time for the Tribe to assimilate.

The Heschtas would need to be at the center of that change, and Devin, as outward-facing Hunt Queen, would be responsible. Garnet had called a meeting of all tribe members for the following day when the sun was at its peak. Then they would put together a plan to overcome and recover from this day's jarring and sad events.

A soft bird call alerted Petrov to the approach of a team. She stopped drumming and hooted in return.

Three shapes materialized from the darkness; Jori, Ara and Jena. They looked weary. All were carrying bows and long staffs. The three young women piled their weapons nearby and sat down near the fire, accepting hot drinks from Petrov.

"Have you seen anything?" Petrov asked

"Nothing. All is quiet." Jori told her. "We took the dead man's body across the river. We laid him at the foot of the cliffs where our other dead lay, and buried him in the manner of the men's tribe, in a trench as deep as my shoulders."

"It was more than he deserved after attacking the children's hut." Jena's tone dripped with anger. "We should have just laid him in the flats for the predators to eat. After all, predator is what he had become. It would be fitting."

"Your anger is understandable, Jena." Petrov began, "But it is not productive. He was born from a woman of our tribe, and spent most of his life with the men's tribe. I know what he did was unfathomable, but he was once one of us. We would do as much for a stranger. That is our way."

"I still have trouble understanding what happened! Why would anyone attack our village?"

Ara's eyes filled, "And with such violence! I heard the awful things they were saying. Why?"

"I do not know, Ara. We may never know." Petrov said sadly. "We can only be glad that they are but a few, and that they are gone."

"At least for now." Jori said sourly. "But we cannot be sure they will not come back again."

"Swain and Lexis are following their tracks to see where they have gone. Your team and Dana's are patrolling upstream and downstream. Tem's team is crossing between you. Devin's nets have been rehung along the river. The village is safe enough for now. The rest will wait for morning. Be grateful no one else was killed."

"But several were injured! Norahjen was shot with an arrow! And Riala's face…" finally, Jena's tears came. She wept quietly, wiping her eyes.

"The healers are taking care of the injured. The loss of food is the biggest problem, and if I know Garnet, she is already forming a plan. We will survive this, and continue to prosper. For now, we can all be kind to one another, and contribute what we can to the effort. All will be well. You will see." Petrov touched the girl's shoulder comfortingly.

Petrov began to drum again, and everyone sat for a time, soaking in the heartbeat. Then Jori put her cup down and stood.

"We should patrol upstream again." The others stood and slung their bows and quivers across their shoulders. "We will return before dawn. If we find trouble, I will screech like an owl."

Petrov nodded, and the three young women disappeared again into the darkness.

When the sun was near mid-sky, the women began to gather. Barde's familiar voice called them to the center house, where Garnet and Devin waited. Wren and her cooks had prepared snacks and cool fruit juice, and the women lounged and enjoyed them as they waited.

"How clever of you, Wren to mix soft cheese with mashed up kartof! And to spread it on these little pieces of crunchy flat bread! This is very good!" Garnet told the hearthwoman.

"We have all been thinking of ways to use the ones that were cooked in the fire while they last. I remembered someone at the Gathering served soft cheese on a crunchy little bread a few turns ago. We added the kartof root and some salt, and a few other secret ingredients." Wren was always happy to elaborate on a new dish.

"Very well done!" Devin agreed. "These are quite tasty!"

When the women were seated and settled, Garnet began.

"Our tribe has suffered a great shock. To be attacked by people who were once our friends and brothers is shocking and sad. But we cannot dwell in this feeling. We must express it, and then move past it. Because of the grave damage to our buildings and the loss of so much stored food, we have much to do to ensure that we will survive the coming winter. When the moon rises this night, we will have a ritual around the main hearth to heal our hearts. Barde will bring messages to those who will be involved. As for repair of our village, we have much to do this day and for many to come. I propose that we assign teams to handle the various tasks. One for the repair of the buildings, one for the gathering of food and materials, one for hunting. Some of you may work with more than one team."

"We have an urgent priority today." Petrov spoke up, surprising Garnet. "The scouts tell me that there is a storm on the way. We must ensure that all our stores are covered from the coming rainstorm before we begin the other tasks."

That pronouncement was greeted with uneasy grumblings and exclamations from the women. To think there could be yet another disaster on the way!

"Thank you for that report, Petrov. I agree that this takes priority. Jori, please go and assess the situation. Make a plan to ensure the safety of our existing supplies, and report back to us. We will all help. In the meantime, we will assign the teams for the other duties." Devin instructed.

"Now, Dana will you lead the repair team to rebuild what has been damaged?"

Garnet asked.

Dana nodded solemnly. "We will repair them before the snow flies."

"Tem, would you please lead out teams of hunters each morning to bring in as much meat as we will need?"

"I will." Tem nodded. She turned to Astaga "Do you have the materials to make extra arrows?"

"I have some nice flexible pine branches, and plenty of flint for the points.

I will make the feathers red for this special hunting." Astaga told her.

"I know a place that is only a two day walk, where there is a large field of kartof plants." Herta told the women. "If a few women will come with me, we can bring back a few drags full."

Devin's eyes narrowed. "Which direction is this field? I do not want any of the teams running into Falcone and his men."

Herta snorted her disgust. "It is to the South. They went to the North. But if you think for one moment that I would be surprised by those inept, smelly…"

Garnet held up a hand, interrupting her "Of course. You could handle them if you needed to, Herta. We know that. Why not leave in a few days, once the storm is passed and things here are underway?"

Herta nodded, still looking disgruntled.

"I will see to it that the last of the harvest is brought in and stored. If we pull together, we will be fine." Garnet said.

"We have survived much leaner times." Norahjen's deep voice soothed them. "We will survive this one as well."

"And do not forget that our friends in the men's tribe would assist also. They have been out tracking the attackers since they heard about the incident. Jonathan thinks he will hear a report from his scouts today." Devin reminded them.

"We have two teams patrolling the area, one upstream and one downstream. And nets with bells have been stretched across the river in several places near the village." Petrov reported." Our teams have reported no intruders or activity at all, except a herd of elk."

"We were lucky that Devin stretched that net when she did. The bells gave us warning. It could have been much worse!" Ara, always the optimist, continued. "Even in this situation, we have much for which to be grateful."

"Grateful???" Marjika spoke for the first time since she fired her arrow into the intruder. "WHAT do we have to be grateful for??" Tears streamed down the woman's face.

"Oh, Marjika, one of the things we are MOST grateful for is YOU!" Ara put her hand gently on the woman's leg. "You saved the children from being taken away or killed by those…those...people. And the dogs fought like warriors and warned you! And the bells warned us all! And the brave Tem, who knocked Falcone unconscious so he could not direct his men! And all of us who fought them off and made them run way!"

There was a murmur in the crowd. Ara had

struck a nerve.

"Yes, we have much to mourn and much to celebrate. We will deal with those feeling this night in sacredness. But for now, we have much to do." Garnet looked up to see Jori's return. "Jori?"

The roof of the grinding hut is intact, but one part of the wall is gone. One of the storage sheds has most of a roof, but the other will need a complete rebuild. I think we can drape skins and fronds over the holes and keep the water out. We will have to secure the patches from the wind, but if we can get everything into those buildings, they will stay dry. Most of the roof of the smoking hut is gone, but the supporting logs remain, so perhaps we can patch that one too. Oh, and the cats have returned." She looked up and signaled that she was finished speaking.

"Thank you, Jori. You and I will take Tem and Dana and Ara and gather materials to make the patches." Devin instructed. "The rest of you, follow Garnet and move our supplies into those three buildings. Anything that will not fit can be moved into this building and hung from the rafters in nets. "

Women began to rise, and move toward the work that needed to be done. Once the building had emptied out, Norahjen asked Ara "What was that about Tem knocking Falcone unconscious?"

Ara laughed. "Oh, you have not heard that story, eh? Well, when they first arrived and confronted the men on that side of the village,

Falcone was screaming insults and pounding his little chest at the line of women who first appeared to defend us. He was so close to Tem's face that his whiskers touched her, and he yelled something at her about how no woman could ever best him in a fight. She never said a word. She just swung her fist and hit him right in the eye. He fell like a dead tree, unconscious. She said 'any woman here is a better fighter than you, little toad.' Then she turned and went after the next one. Falcone missed the whole fight and had to be dragged away by his men when they fled."

Norahjen laughed so hard she had a coughing fit. "Good on Tem." She said. "Now maybe he will go far away and stay there. I am almost sorry I ever found him."

"And how were you injured, Norahjen?" the girl asked.

"Oh, one of them was trying to get into the temple. Astaga and I blocked his path. He raised his spear toward me, and I swung my walking stick and knocked the spear downward. It caught my leg. Before he could pull his spear back, Astaga hit him with a bone club and he dropped to the ground. She dragged him to the river and rolled him down the bank. He floated away downstream."

"I am sorry you were injured." Ara said, touching the big woman's bandages.

"I guess I am lucky I deflected the blow. If the spear had hit me in the chest, I could be dead now. This leg, at least, will heal in time. Now you go on and help the others. I am fine here by the fire. Anna will check on me later." The girl hesitated. Norahjen smiled softly, and patted the girl's arm. "It will be alright, Ara. Go on now. You are needed elsewhere."

Winter 1986 C.E.

I stomped the snow off my boots on the old wooden porch, and carried yet another armful of wood into the house. After dumping the wood in the bin I removed my wet coat and hung it near the stove to dry for the next trip outside. The twisted willow rocking chair groaned as I fell into it, grateful for a moment of rest.

Anna handed me a tin cup of coffee, and sat across from me, watching me sip it. I was content to watch the fire and savor the warm drink. We sat that way, silent for a while.

"You are changing." She said finally. "You are developing patience."

I smiled, savoring the rare compliment.

"You once asked me what had happened to our tribe…why there are so few of us left."

"Yes. The way you describe it, there were thousands of us at one time. Why did our tribe die out?" I asked.

"Our tribe is not dead, it is diluted." She said sadly. "There are but a few of us who have the pure blood of our people. The rest are descendants of those who were carried away and forced into what they called 'marriage'. Many were kept by the Gols. But others were traded like bags of corn to whatever traveler who could pay the price. But even those with a remnant of our blood still feel the pull toward our people. I think those are the ones that attend your Meesheegan summer mu-sik festival."

I suspected strongly that she was correct. "How did this happen?" I asked, afraid of the answer and thinking that I already knew it.

"We had been defending ourselves against the Gols for generations. After the idiot Falcone was run off, he travelled back to his native tribe and told them where to find us. Over the next many years, we would suffer periodic attacks by bands of them. Sometimes we drove them off with nothing. Sometimes they did damage. Many Heschtas were killed defending the village. Our allied men's tribe advised us to move around, to go back to travelling with the seasons. But we refused to leave the home that we had worked so hard to build." She paused, looking down at the floor.

She was gathering herself, I thought. She

looked me in the eye. "Then one summer, while many of our women were away at festival, they came in large numbers. They killed scores of our women, burned the village almost to the ground, and carried off the young women and children."

"When the travelers came back from the summer festival, they found decimation.. The only building intact was the temple. When you are ready, I will tell you the whole tale. But be forewarned, it is ugly and sad."

"Will you not tell me all of it now? I have these nightmares….perhaps they are memories."

"They may be, But no, young one. It is not yet time for that. Leave the horrors of the past where they are for now. You will learn the truth in time." I had never heard her voice take on a more gentle tone.

I let the silence settle, tears streaming from my eyes, and hers. The only sound for a time was the crackling of the flames in the stove. At last, she wiped her eyes and went on.

"They buried those who were lost in the ground, and with as much ceremony as they could muster. The Hearth Queen kept the staff of the Hunt Queen as a reminder." She nodded toward a corner of the cottage. "It stands in the corner, over there. It has been carried by every Hunt Queen since. I and you are direct descendants of that Hearth Queen."

I got up and walked to the corner she indicated. Leaning into the corner was a tall staff, darkened by age and the oil of many hands. I looked over and received a nod of permission. I reached out slowly, grasping the leather grip and pulling it to me. My hand tingled. "I can feel hands covering mine." I said softly. The old woman nodded, her eyes shining.

"It now belongs to you, Tem. When you leave here, you will take it with you as a reminder of who we are." Touched beyond words, I returned the staff to its place and returned to mine.

"The survivors wintered in the caves above the river, eating only what they could hunt. And in the Spring, they began to rebuild."

"So the tribe survived the winter?" I asked

"Yes, but there were not many left. And the village was never the same. After a few turns of the wheel, the women decided to move. To find another place that did not hold the terrible memories of returning home to find so much destruction."

I sighed into the pause.

"The women burned the village to cleanse the ground. They left only the temple standing, and they travelled here to these mountains, and stayed."

I have never forgotten that day, or the look on the old woman's face as she told me the tale. And to this day, every time I enter a ritual, I can feel my ancestors' hands, covering mine on that staff. They stay with me and protect me as I continue the tradition of service of the Heschtas, the Guardians of our tribe.

WINTER, 3778 B.C.E

Swain fed another stick into the little fire and moved her wet boots closer so they would dry out overnight. She had gathered a pile of dry sticks and set them aside as she swept the area under the towering pine tree, clearing space for her shelter. She had lined the ground with soft pine boughs to insulate her from the cold of the ground, and laid her sleeping fur on top of them.

The lowest branches of the old tree reached almost to the ground, and would provide a roof and a wind break. She placed her pack near her head, up against the massive tree's trunk, to use as a pillow. And she laid her bow and spear nearby within easy reach. Her labrys lay alongside the little pile of wood, ready to chop the long branches into smaller, usable chunks.

She had picked a place almost to the top of the hill where she could see the smoke from the village in the distance and keep an eye on the approaches up- and down-stream. She had built a wall of snow along the outside. The berm would shield her further from the wind and serve to insulate her little nest. Normally, she would not have made such an elaborate shelter for a scout nest. But her assignment would keep her here for five nights until Nita came to relieve her, and someone would be sleeping here all winter, so she would try to make it as comfortable and warm as possible.

Now that the deep snow had fallen, the strategy they had used of patrolling up and down river had been changed. The Heschtas had held a council and talked it over. They all believed that once the snow was deep, the chance of a raid was diminished. Also, walking in high snow was dangerous and difficult for the guardians.
They had decided that they would set up three outposts; one upstream, one downstream and one across the flats in the hills, where Swain was now. The stony cliffs that sheltered the village from the east prevented any approach from that direction.

Women would be assigned to scout in the shelters for turns lasting five nights, and then would be relieved by the next person's turn. The women would have ten sleeps back in the village before taking another turn. This way, no one would have to spend the entire winter out in the cold. They picked three teams of three for the assignments. Swain, Herta and Jori were the first team to go out.

While there was still some daylight, Swain climbed up the branches of the old tree to get a good view of the surrounding area. From up here, she could see any movement near the village. Seeing nothing alarming, she climbed down and began to warm some water for tea to drink with her travel rations. Tomorrow she would set up snares. Perhaps she would catch something and have fresh meat. She hung the pouches of medicines and signal powder from an overhead branch to the side of her bed. Yes, she thought, this would be a comfortable nest. She sipped her tea thinking of ways to further improve it without making it visible to passing humans.

Tomorrow, she would set up a signal fire nearby. The plan was that each outpost would have a bonfire ready to light in case an approaching party was spotted. The pouches of signal powders would be kept full; red smoke would mean a party of unknown or dangerous people, green would signal friends approaching. Someone would be assigned to be at the Heschtas' fire at all times, watching in case a signal came.

Norahjen insisted on that assignment. Her injured knee prevented her from doing any walking yet, but she stubbornly performed any tasks she could think of as useful. Her demeanor was angry and abrupt; a far cry from the steady gentle woman the Tribe had followed for so much of Devin's life.

~~~~

Devin walked over to the storage huts, where Dana and her team were finishing up the roof of the second building. She stood for a few moments, watching the women work. It appeared that they were close to completion. She gave a soft whistle. Dana's face appeared over the edge of the wall.

"Come on up and have a closer look" Dana offered.

Devin climbed up and perched on one of the support logs at the top of the wall.

Dana indicated the thatching pattern, and explained "We have braided the edges of the thatching pieces together. That will make them stronger when the winds are gusting. See?"

Devin examined the piece that Dana indicated, and was impressed. Having all the pieces connected would indeed make for a stronger roof during the spring storms. "Good idea!" she smiled at her friend.

"Actually, it is something Ara talked about. She said she noticed last summer that the wind had a harder time blowing larger items than smaller ones. So by connecting the pieces together, we are making a larger, stronger piece that is harder for the wind to lift. And look over here," she indicated a small opening on the wall, just below the roof line. We put these openings on all four sides, so if the wind gets into the hut, it will have someplace to go without lifting the roof off."

Devin inspected the little opening. The women had stretched a tiny net across the opening. That would keep out the birds and flying insects, but allow the wind to pass through. "Excellent!" she exclaimed. "I want Herta to see this when she returns from her scouting trip, so she can add it to the permanent records. It is a very smart way to build! Perhaps you will teach about it at the Gathering this summer?"

Dana laughed, enjoying the praise. "We will see about that when the summer comes, old friend. We still have to make sure we get through this winter first."

As Devin made her way around the circle toward the Heschta's fire, she heard raised voices. She hurried toward the angry sounds.

"I don't care if you have already cut up every branch under the sun into tiny little bits! Bring me a labrys and some small logs!" Norahjen was standing up, leaning on the tall stack of rocks that the Heschtas used as a work top. Her face was red from exertion and annoyance.

Jena, a healer's apprentice stood nearby. She was holding a crutch and looking quite flustered. "But, Anna said…"

"Anna is a mother goat! I MUST do as much as I can to stretch the muscle!"

Devin's arrival brought a relieved look from the girl. "What is happening?" she asked.

"Now don't YOU start!" Norahjen barked.

"About what?" Devin kept her voice even and her tone casual. "I just came because I heard someone yelling."

"Oh, Devin!" Jena wailed plaintively. "Anna says that Norahjen should not stand for long periods or do anything strenuous. And she..."

"All I want to do" the older woman interrupted, "is to chop up a couple of logs. I am looking for pieces that I can carve. The sooner someone gets me some wood, the sooner I can sit!" Norahjen's exasperation had exhausted her. She was leaning heavily on the rocks now.

Devin turned to the girl and made a 'go away' motion, smiling kindly. She took the crutch from the girl's hand. "I will assist her, Jena." Gratefully, the girl escaped.

Devin turned and silently handed the crutch to her mentor. Her look would accept no argument. "Sit down and wait here. I will get a few logs to look over. No sense in you using your energy to stand while you wait."

Norahjen sighed heavily, and sat down near the fire. Would this young one have any idea how she was feeling? She thought not. Devin was a good girl, but did not have enough life experience to understand the confusing jumble of Norahjen's feelings. She fervently hoped that Devin would have tact and sense enough to forego a lecture.

"I need three or four useable pieces, about the size of your forearm." She instructed Devin.

Calmer, she sat down to await the delivery.

Devin went behind the house, and returned with several small logs for the old scout to look over.

"What are you making?" Devin asked.

"Whistle pipes. Remember Mare?" Norahjen spoke as she inspected each piece of wood. The feel of the grain in her hands calmed her heart.

"Yes. She worked at the hearth at the Gathering last summer. From a place called Eire."

"That is her." Norahjen's voice had returned to normal. "She showed me how to make wooden pipes that make a whistling sound when you blow through them. They can be heard for a fair distance. I thought we needed another way to warn the village in case it rains or is too foggy to see signal smoke. There. These four will do for a start."

Devin rose and threw the unchosen logs over near the fire circle. She picked up the pieces Norahjen had selected and laid them next to the work top. Then she turned and extended her hand to the woman. "Come on, then."

Norahjen grasped her hand and pulled herself upright, glancing at the girl's face to assess if there was concern, or worse yet, pity. Seeing no judgments in the eyes of her student, she took the crutch from Devin. She hobbled over to the work table and picked up the first piece.

Devin suppressed an urge to assist, knowing that her mentor needed to struggle through and accomplish something. So she sat down and poked at the fire with a stick. Her dogs came ambling over for some affection. She ruffled their ears, smiling. Then it came to her.

"Trooper?" she said tentatively, using her affectionate childhood name for Norahjen.

The woman looked up, suspicious. "What. You are not going to start now too, are you?"

"No. But I would like you to have a chance to see the new scout nests. I want to make sure no one forgot anything. "

"Well I cannot very well walk that far yet. Are you planning to carry me all that way like an infant? What more must I endure?" Norahjen was getting wound up again.

"NO, no! But I just had an idea. What if we leash the dogs to a sled, and you can ride it out to see the three scout nests? We can rig up leashes for you to hold, so you can pull on them to get the dogs to stop when you need to."

Norahjen looked up, speculative. "Do you think they would do it?"

"I think so." Devin was smiling now. They pull the sleds up when we are hill riding, and the black one even jumps on when the sleds are going downhill."

"Yes, but that is a game to them. This would be work."

"Everything I have ever taught them has started as a game. Because that is how YOU taught ME!" Devin was excited now. "You keep working on your whistle pipes. By the time you are finished, I may have something arranged so you can deliver them in person!"

"I will not hold my breath." Norahjen grumbled. If Devin could make this happen, it WOULD restore some mobility. More than one way to skin a rabbit, she thought, smiling to herself for the first time since the accident. Perhaps she had been looking at this all wrong. Perhaps it was just another challenge to be met by a smart and strong warrior. Yes, she promised herself, she would meet this challenge as she had all the others in her lifetime, with bravery and optimism.

Devin hugged her, "Can I trust you to sit when you are tired? Or should I find someone to supervise you?" Receiving the expected growl in return, she took her leave. Devin knew that the combination of some time alone and a useful task would help the scout regain her balance. And if she had trouble, there were people close by in the Heschta's hut who would hear her call for help.

Devin made her way to the healer's house. She wanted to calm Jena and give Anna some advice. She found Jena, sitting outside the house, crying. She patted the girl's shoulder and went inside.

"Anna." She said. The healer was bent over her small fire, stirring something that smelled like pine needles.

"That stubborn old woman has sent two different apprentices back here in tears." Anna sounded annoyed.

"I know." Devin agreed. "She is having a difficult time. How is her injury healing?"

"It is healing, but the damage to her knee is permanent. Right now, she can only manage a few steps at a time without help. She will eventually be able to walk short distances over flat ground, but will not be able to climb or carry much."

"To a woman who has lived as a hunter and scout, this is a very big change." Devin said. "For much of her life, she has been the strongest, the fastest, the best hunter, the wisest leader. I doubt she will even be able to get to the Gathering this summer; and certainly not without help. She is grappling with her future usefulness, even her identity."

Anna looked thoughtful. "I have been focused on the physical injury. There are emotional wounds, too, that must be looked after."

"Yes." Devin agreed. "I think we must allow her to do as much as she feels she is able to do. We must allow her to struggle with the injury as though it were an enemy until she and it come to some understanding."

"But if she does too much, she will do further damage to the knee." Anna said.

"How much more damage could she do, really?" Devin asked.

"She could prevent herself from ever walking anywhere or standing up at all." Anna explained.

"But if she loses hope, she loses everything." Devin's gentle voice became persuasive "I know

Trooper. She would not want to continue to live if she could not serve. She must work through this in her own way."

"It is the same struggle all women have when they reach a certain age, you know." Anna said; her tone calmer.

"But most women have several seasons to adjust. The changes come gradually for most. For Trooper, it happened in moments. It is a shock. It will take time for her to figure it out." Devin said. "And a little subtle help."

"What are you suggesting?" Anna asked.

"Just this: let her do as much as she thinks she can. If you want to keep someone nearby in case of emergency, just make them less…visible. If Norahjen feels like you are mothering her, she will become surly again. She needs to feel like she is making progress on her own."

"I will agree, but only if you get her to promise to sit when she is tired." Anna sighed.

"I already have her word that she will rest when she tires. And she is close enough to the Heschtas that they will hear her if she calls."

Across the compound, Garnet and Wren were assessing their remaining food stores. They had spent the end of the harvest season gathering the remaining crops. They had also sent out parties to gather nuts (for grinding into flour), and cattails (the bulbs were used for insulation and kindling, and the roots were edible). They had re-strung the hanging nets once the hut roofs were repaired. Everyone had also been hunting and/or fishing to bolster their supplies of protein. Now that the deep snow had come, they had to make plans to make it last until spring.

"The cabbage crop was good. And we have lots of onions." Wren was saying. "We will have to make sure that the apprentices turn them in the nets periodically, to keep the heads cool and dry on all sides. If we add cabbage and kartof and onion to the pot, we can make soups that are filling and nutritious, and that will help the remaining kartof supply last longer."

"   I agree." Garnet nodded her head, "We will be short of other greens soon. We will have to go out and look for the winter greens. You know the spot where the reindeer find them. And we do have carrots. They last longer into the cold other things. We should save the carrots for later, when the more perishable vegetables run out."

"It was very smart of Riala to hang them by their tops over strings." Wren was impressed with the girl's determination and recovery. "She said she got the idea from hanging fish in the smokehouse."

"I am very proud of her, you know. She is my most promising apprentice. I think she will take my place one day." Wren confided.

"I am glad. She was always a good girl. And she was brave in the face of danger."

They entered the second hut, where the workers were just finishing the roof.

"What about flour? Have we been able to recover much?" Garnet asked.

"Not as much as we would normally use. I think we should refrain from making the sticky treats and fruit pies until Solstice." Wren advised.

"Why then?" Garnet was curious about the cook's logic.

"If we withhold them for a while, it will seem like a bigger treat. And it will be a welcome change at Solstice, just when everyone is getting bored with cabbage and onions." Wren told the leader. "And I also suggest that we only make flat bread every third day instead of every day. I think that will stretch the flour out as long as possible."

"Seems like a good plan. How are the cheese stores?"

"Most of the cheeses were unharmed. A few retained a smokier taste than the others. I think they were closer to that wall."

"But we will have enough then?" Garnet asked.

"Oh, I think so. There will be plenty of meat. We even sent a few rounds of cheese along with some smoked fish for the gifts when Jonathan and the men went south. Even though it may stress our stores of the cheese, we wanted them to know we will still be their friends when they come back."

"Yes." Garnet agreed. That was a good plan. So it seems with a little judicious management that we will survive the winter."

"Oh, there will be lacks, and the hunters and fishers will have to keep at it all winter. I expect some will grumble about the lack of bread and pies, but none should starve." Wren told her.

Downstream, Jori had stopped working on her scout shelter. She stood, looking toward the flats across from the village, trying to make out what was coming toward her. She could clearly see Devin's lanky form running along, and beside Devin were ....dogs? Yes! The dogs ran alongside Devin. And they were pulling a drag! She shook her head, smiling. What was Devin up to now, she wondered. They seemed to be coming directly toward Jori's shelter.

Jori swung her water pot over the fire, ready to make Devin a hot drink when she arrived, and scrounged around the ashes for a couple of bones for Devin's companions.

By the time the water began to boil, Devin and the dogs had arrived.

"Hello!" She called to Devin, bending to scratch the ears of the dogs as they greeted her. "What is this new adventure you are having?"

Devin sat near the fire, grinning. "I am training the dogs to pull a sled on the snow." She explained. "Now at first, the sled will be empty. But as we go, I will add weight. And then eventually, a person."

Handing Devin a hot cup of tea. Jori asked "A person? You want a person to ride on the sled and for the dogs to pull them places? Why?"

Devin took a sip of the hot liquid. "To help Trooper get around to more places than her lame leg will take her."

Jori grinned at her mentor. "AH! What a wonderful idea! Ara told me that Norahjen's leg would prevent her from long travel. Do you think we can figure out how to direct the dogs and get them to stop? It is one thing to get them to run…it is another to get them to run in a particular direction."

"They do understand a few words. And they come when I whistle. Perhaps we can teach them one sound for left and another for right, and one for stop and go. I notice you said we…..will you help me try?"

"Of course I will! As soon as you and they are rested, we can start." She strolled over to inspect the sled. "I would build a little platform, here toward the back. If you are sitting flat on the bottom of this sled, you cannot see the terrain that is coming. Sitting up a little higher would give you better visibility."

"Good idea. And the platform itself will add a little weight. But if the person sits up too high, it will make the sled unstable. We will have to add width…."Devin rubbed her chin thoughtfully…..how about…" she jumped up and found a straight stick and laid it alongside the sled, about a foot from the main body. "One of these on each side would stabilize the sled and if the bottom of the rail is sharp, it will glide easily over the ice...."

"Yes! And we can lash them to the sides of the sled with sinew....that will make it much faster too!" Jori grinned, knowing that together, they could make this work for their teacher and friend.

EPILOGUE
WINTER SOLSTICE MORNING 3779 B.C.E.

"Where is Norahjen?" Garnet's impatient tone made Devin wince. "We cannot light the new year's fire without her. She is eldest."

"She knows. She will come." Devin consoled. "We have the fire lain in the main hearth. She will simply have to add the spark from the sacred torch."

"The torch has been burning since midnight. It will not last all day." Garnet grumbled. "Ever since you built her that sled, she has been darting about from place to place...and now that we need her...."

"She knows the tradition. She will be here shortly."

"And the women are beginning to gather at the main

house."

"I will go and have a look. Come. Let's join the Tribe outside." Devin coaxed, leading the Hearth Queen out of their shared hut and toward the village center. Both looked up simultaneously as the clatter and barking of the dogs approached. "Here she is now, see?"

Norahjen arrived, gliding quickly into the center of the village on her sled. She pulled at the tethers, and the dogs slowed. "Stop" she commanded. The dogs obediently came to a stop and promptly lay down. Their panting faces appeared to be smiling. "Good dogs."

Trooper stood, picking up her walking stick in one hand and a few pieces of dried meat from her pouch in the other. She patted each dog and gave it a reward, then turned to the Queens.

"How are the scouts?" Devin asked.

"All are warm and safe." Norahjen replied. "Swain has even caught a few rabbits for a stew. They all report quiet. No movement from any direction."

"Thank you, Trooper. Are you ready to light the new fire?"

"I am."

Garnet went into the main hearth and came out immediately, holding the ancient torch. She walked to Norahjen and said loudly; "Mother, as our eldest and wisest member, will you light the fire for this new turn of the seasons and speak your wish for our Tribe?"

"I will" Norahjen took the torch from Garnet, handed

her stick to Devin, and walked unaided (though haltingly) to the main hearth where the new fire had been set up for her.

"As elder of this Tribe I will speak my gratitude for every member of this village. I am grateful that our Tribe possesses the courage to face danger, the compassion to help others, the resourcefulness to deal with challenges, the love to care for one another, and the respect of our world and all the beings who reside here. I am proud of each of you for your skills and your sense."

She raised the torch high and slowly brought it down to the kindling that waited as she said "May this turn of the seasons bring us continued joy, safety and health. May our Tribe forever endure, no matter what comes. May we be fruitful and carry our traditions bravely and happily into the future."

As she finished speaking, she touched the torch to the kindling; a merry fire began to dance.

www.ingramcontent.com/pod-product-compliance
Lightning Source LLC
Chambersburg PA
CBHW071243130626
46556CB00003B/1137